"Why All The Time?"

Tony growled at her.

"Hospital patients usually like to be cheered up. But for you, Sergeant Griffin, I'll try to be more glum, if it'll make you feel better."

"What would make me feel better, Delia, is for you to leave me alone and let me suffer in peace." The incessant pounding in his head was making his tongue sharper than usual. But he hadn't wanted to deal with Delia last night when he was in full control of his faculties, and he surely wasn't in the mood to deal with her when he was in a hospital bed.

If Delia Pryde knew what was good for her, she'd scoot out of his life. If she insisted on hanging around, he was either going to keep snapping at her . . . or take her to bed. . . .

Dear Reader,

Q. What does our heroine know about the hero when she first meets him?
A. Not much!

His personality, background, family—his entire life—is a total mystery. I started to think that the heroine never *truly* knows what's in store for her when she first sees the hero. In fact, *her* life from that moment on can be likened to an adventure with a ''mysterious'' man. And it's from these thoughts that our Valentine's Day promotion, MYSTERY MATES, was born. After all, who *is* this guy and what *is* he looking for?

Each of our heroes this month is a certain type of man, as I'm sure you can tell from the title of each February Desire book. The *Man of the Month* by Raye Morgan is *The Bachelor* . . . a man who never dreamed he'd have anything to do with—*children!* Cait London brings us *The Cowboy,* Ryanne Corey *The Stranger,* Beverly Barton *The Wanderer* and from Karen Leabo comes *The Cop.*

Peggy Moreland's hero, *The Rescuer,* is a very special man indeed. For while his story is completely fictitious, the photo on the cover is that of a Houston, Texas, fire fighter. Picked from a calendar the Houston Fire Department creates for charity, this man is truly a hero.

So, enjoy our MYSTERY MATES. They're sexy, they're handsome, they're lovable . . . and they're only from Silhouette Desire.

Lucia Macro
Senior Editor

KAREN LEABO

THE COP

SILHOUETTE *Desire*

™ Published by Silhouette Books New York

America's Publisher of Contemporary Romance

This book is dedicated to:

Sgt. James L. Chandler
Lt. David M. Davis, Jr.
Sgt. Randy L. Hooper
Sgt. Danny Lawson
Officer Ed McAdoo
Cheryl Palmer

and all of the hardworking men and women
of the Dallas Police Department

SILHOUETTE BOOKS
300 East 42nd St., New York, N.Y. 10017

THE COP

ISBN: 0-373-05767-9

First Silhouette Books printing February 1993

Printed in the U.S.A.

Books by Karen Leabo

Silhouette Desire

Close Quarters #629
Lindy and the Law #676
Unearthly Delights #704
The Cop #767

Silhouette Romance

Roses Have Thorns #648
Ten Days in Paradise #692
Domestic Bliss #707
Full Bloom #731
Smart Stuff #764
Runaway Bride #797
The Housewarming #848
A Changed Man #886

KAREN LEABO

credits her fourth-grade teacher with initially sparking her interest in creative writing. She was determined at an early age to have her work published. When she was in the eighth grade, she wrote a children's book and convinced her school yearbook publisher to put it in print.

Karen was born and raised in Dallas. She has worked as a magazine art director, a free-lance writer and a textbook editor, but now she keeps herself busy full-time writing about romance.

A Letter from the Author

Dear Reader:

When I met Rory, an accountant from Ireland who was in town to audit my employer's books, the sparks flew. We both felt it, though nothing was said.

That evening, a group of us took Rory to a local club. He paid me no special attention, as this would have been highly improper. Delicate negotiations were in progress between his company in Ireland and mine. But I felt a definite undercurrent of electricity.

Gradually the group dispersed until only Rory and I remained. The moment we were alone, our eyes met and we laughed in sheer relief.

We danced to every slow song until the club closed. It was like we'd known each other forever. Unwilling to part, we went to his hotel.

Don't jump to conclusions! A few lascivious thoughts *did* cross our minds, but soon Rory would return to Ireland, and we would never see each other again. Neither of us wanted to trivialize the bond we'd formed with a tawdry one-night stand.

So we talked, laughed and stuffed ourselves with his "welcome basket" of fruit and cheese.

At 7:30 a.m. I awoke in a panic. We had fallen asleep! Rory had a breakfast meeting scheduled with my boss at eight, so there was time for nothing more than one impassioned farewell kiss.

As I was leaving the hotel, my boss was arriving. I ducked my head and hoped for the best. Preoccupied, he never saw me. The forbidden tryst remained a secret.

Sincerely,

Karen Leabo

One

Something was up. Sergeant Tony Griffin detected a strange mood permeating the Detail Room as the officers shuffled in and found their customary chairs.

It wasn't just the usual tensions that preceded the Saturday night eleven-to-seven shift. Cops on first watch, Tony included, were always a little more wary, a little more keyed up. Bad things happened during "deep nights," especially in the neighborhoods where Tony cruised.

The restlessness in the air this night, however, was something different.

It was Tony's turn to call roll from the front of the room and assign his officers to their various duties. As he read off the names, he could sense the anticipation among the other sergeants sitting beside him. Even Lieutenant Lapp, his immediate superior, kept put-

ting his hand over his mouth to hide a clandestine
smile.

What the hell . . . ?

Whatever the joke was, Tony seemed to be the only
one not in on it. Or was he just getting paranoid in his
old age? At thirty-five, he was one of the more sea-
soned sergeants at this station.

He read off a list of routine announcements re-
garding arrests made during the previous shift as well
as personnel and policy changes. He distributed sub-
poenas to officers ordered to appear in court. All the
while, he kept expecting the joke to spring, but nothing happened.

Detail took less than five minutes—not much going
on. When business was finished, Lieutenant Lapp,
seated to Tony's far right, mumbled a quick, "Y'all be
careful out there," dismissing the officers. Then he
turned to the three sergeants and let loose the wicked
grin he'd been holding back. "One of you guys is in
for an *interesting* evening."

"Why is that, sir?" Tony responded, playing the
straight man as always to his superior's offbeat sense
of humor. Humor had its place, Tony supposed, but
not when it came to police work. That was the only
complaint he had about Lapp. He was a helluva smart
cop and a good supervisor, but he didn't take things
seriously sometimes.

Then again, no one seemed to be serious, he thought
as he looked first at one, then the other of his two fellow sergeants. Hank Smith was smiling as if he was
about to win the lottery, and Tommy Hidalgo was
laughing like a hyena.

"You didn't see her?" Smith asked Tony. "I thought *everyone* saw her. I mean, you could hardly miss her."

"Miss who?" Then his stomach sank. "Oh, no, not another Ride Along?" *Please, God, no.* So far Tony had managed to avoid participating in the Ride Along program, an asinine idea if he'd ever heard one.

"A Ride Along," Lapp confirmed, still grinning like a dog anticipating a particularly juicy bone. "And a knockout, at that. Keys, please." Smith and Hidalgo had their key rings ready to toss into a brown paper sack the lieutenant held. Tony forced himself to surrender his. He had a bad feeling that tonight his number was up.

With great ceremony Lapp reached into the bag and selected a set of keys. Tony wasn't too surprised to see it was his.

"You lucky dog," said Smith. "Why couldn't it be me?"

"You can have her," Tony grumbled as they all walked out the door together. "I don't *want* a civilian riding with me while I'm working, especially not a woman."

"No way, Griffin," Lapp said. "You can't weasel out of this one. We've all done it two or three times. It's your turn."

Tony just shook his head in disgust. Ordinary civilians riding around in patrol cars alongside an officer—Ride Along was insane! The program was designed to "foster community awareness" among Dallas citizens, to show them exactly how the police department functioned under real-life circumstances. All it accomplished was to allow "Miami Vice" wanna be's to live out their macho fantasies while distracting police officers from their jobs.

Or in this case, maybe it was a "Cagney and Lacey" fan.

"She's waiting for you in the TV lounge," Lapp said. "Her name's Delia Pryde. And you better be nice. You know Chief Shenniker doesn't like to hear complaints from the Ride Alongs."

Tony gave a resigned sigh. "Understood."

He strode down the hall toward the lounge, an area normally reserved for officers but where visitors sometimes were allowed to wait. He tamped down his annoyance and prepared himself to be *nice*.

She was alone in the lounge, leaning against a wall and flipping through a magazine. But even if she'd been surrounded by others, she would have claimed Tony's immediate attention. She was clad in softly faded jeans that hugged her slender legs and hips. Her fuzzy, baby blue sweater draped over full, rounded breasts and gathered loosely at her narrow waist. The crowning glory was her hair—not quite red, not brown, not blond—pulled up in a loose ponytail of cascading bronze curls.

This ethereal fantasy wanted to ride around in South Dallas? No wonder everyone was laughing.

She saw him then and smiled with the radiance of an atomic flash, and in a heartbeat Tony understood why the other sergeants had been so eager to have their keys drawn out of the sack. With her upturned nose, crystalline blue eyes and that smile, she was more than beautiful. She was . . . she was . . .

Who *cares* what she looks like, he thought grimly, annoyed by his own unprofessional reaction to her. He

still didn't want her riding next to him during a grueling first watch. What if something happened to her?

One of his worst nightmares, one that came true
from time to time, was breaking bad news to an innocent victim's parents, or husband or wife. The task
was even more bitter when he knew the tragedy could
have been prevented.

Well, if anything happened to this butterfly of a
woman, it wouldn't be on his head, he thought, grit-
ting his teeth. Allowing her to ride with him wasn't his
idea.

She stepped toward him, hand outstretched, smile
still firmly in place. "I'm Delia Pryde. Please call me
Delia. And you're Sergeant—" she peered at his name
tag "—Griffin."

He took the hand reluctantly, gave it a perfunctory
shake, then let go. Still, though he'd touched it for
perhaps one second, the feel of her hand left a strong
impression on him. *Soft, warm, strong . . .*

"What should I call you?" she asked.

"Sergeant Griffin." He refused to let her charm
him. Too bad his hormones didn't understand that.
His physical response to her was purely male, and his
emotional reaction primitive. He wanted to protect
her, shield her, from life's grim realities. "I don't
suppose I could talk you out of . . ." He appraised the
anticipatory look on her angelic face and shook his
head. "No, guess not. This way, then."

You can get through this, he coached himself as he
headed out the main doors toward the Southeast Station's front canopy, where his car was parked. A lot of
other sergeants had survived Ride Alongs, and some
had even enjoyed the experience. Hank Smith had said
that a civilian's company offered a fresh perspective,

a diversion from the ordinary. As if any of them needed a diversion when they never knew what sordid mess they might stumble across around the next corner.

He hadn't checked to see if she was following; he didn't have to. He could smell her. He could smell the innocence that clung to her as surely as the aura of her intriguing and very feminine perfume. She was in for an eye-opening experience tonight.

He jerked open the driver's door of his patrol car, then recoiled as a familiar and not very welcome scent of another kind assaulted his nose. "Oh, for cryin' out—"

"What?" Delia asked, still waiting for him to unlock the passenger door.

"I hate it when the previous shift tows around some drunk in my patrol car and leaves the mess for me to clean up."

He opened the back door and found the source of the odor—a towel. At least someone had made an attempt to contain the mess. At least it wasn't all over his upholstery.

"What's that?" Delia asked with a delicate wrinkle of her nose as Tony withdrew the soiled towel.

"You don't want to know," he replied dryly before turning to find a garbage can.

As Delia watched him walk away holding the towel at arm's length, she felt the first pricklings of apprehension. She quickly pushed them aside. For heaven's sake.... It was just a dirty towel and a noxious odor, no worse than what any parent with a sick child might face. Once upon a time, such unsavory things were a routine part of her existence, though she'd all but forgotten them over the past eighteen years. Now she was making a conscious decision to reacquaint herself with the seamier side of life. If she expected to succeed, she'd better toughen up.

She focused her attention on her companion for the evening and smiled as her optimism returned. His confident swagger and an economy of words marked him as a self-proclaimed tough guy, but the image was probably accurate. His tall, broad-shouldered, flat-bellied body, at least, inspired confidence in his physical abilities, and the intelligence behind the watchful dark eyes proclaimed him a man of deep thoughts as well as quick, effective action.

She'd hardly exchanged two words with him, but she instinctively knew he was good at his job. Whatever happened tonight, she would be riding with one of Dallas's finest. *And one of Dallas's finest-looking,* she added. His thick, unruly black hair was combed back from a high forehead, accentuating finely chiseled facial features. As he returned to the patrol car she studied that face, noting the expressive eyebrows, the straight, regular nose, the strong jaw and the mouth—especially the mouth. His lips were full and well shaped, just made for...

Delia quickly censored that thought.

He probably had straight, white teeth, she mused, but he hadn't yet given her a glimpse of them. It would take a smile to do that, and somehow Delia imagined a smile would be hard-won from this man.

Sergeant Griffin unlocked her door with the push of a button, and she climbed into the patrol car as he did. The vestiges of an unpleasant odor remained. She coughed, but refrained from commenting. It was a crisp autumn evening. Maybe if they rode with the windows open for a while, the odor would dissipate. She started to crack her window.

"Don't do that," Griffin said, immediately halting her.

He started the engine, switched on the on-board computer, opened the vents, adjusted mirrors, all without another word. She might have been invisible for all the attention he paid her.

"What do we do first?" she asked brightly.

"*We* don't do anything," he replied as he pulled the car out of the parking lot. "I'm on my way to answer one of the seventeen calls left over from the last shift. You're going to sit there and . . . observe."

"Yes, I understand that. But you'll answer questions, won't you? I mean, this is supposed to be an educational process, right?"

His hands tightened almost imperceptibly around the steering wheel as his wary eyes surveyed the dark streets. "Yeah, all right. I'll answer questions."

Delia decided she'd better spend her quota of questions judiciously. Sergeant Tony Griffin was apt to get balky if she tried his patience. So she watched the scenery, such as it was—weedy, vacant lots, hollow-eyed apartment buildings, convenience stores with barred windows, a deserted gas station—and carefully selected her words.

"Don't sergeants normally supervise rather than go on calls themselves?"

He turned, and for an instant his attention was exclusively devoted to her before he returned his eyes to the road. Apparently the question had taken him off guard.

"Normally, yes. But it's a busy night. As long as I'm cruising the neighborhood, I might as well check on this burglar alarm that went off—'' he consulted the computer screen ''—more than an hour ago.''

He wasn't what Delia would call "chatty." But at least he'd spoken a couple of complete sentences to her. If she asked a few more questions, maybe she could get him to open up. Otherwise, this was going to be a tedious eight hours.

"What if..." But she didn't get the chance to complete her intended question. Griffin had turned the car into a driveway on a residential street and braked sharply.

"Wait here," he ordered as he climbed swiftly out of the car and started toward the house.

"Like hell," Delia muttered, following him up the front steps of the old house. She didn't intend to spend the entire shift staring at the dashboard.

The structure was dark, forbidding. "What are you doing?" she called in a loud stage whisper.

He halted abruptly and turned on her. "I told you to stay in the car."

"I thought I was supposed to follow you wherever you went."

"Subject to my approval, which you do not have, so get back in the car."

"Why? There's no danger here."

"How the hell do you know that? It just so happens that a burglar alarm went off here. Inside, the place could be crawling with armed crackheads. Now get back in the car."

"Well, when you put it like that..." Delia withdrew a few paces, but she didn't return to the car. "Will you call to me when you know it's clear?"

He ignored her.

She waited by the car, ready to dive inside if she heard shots, but her gaze remained glued to Griffin. After knocking on the door to no avail, he scanned around with his flashlight, peeked through a front window, then edged around to the side of the porch. Apparently he saw nothing there, because he descended the stairs and walked around to the driveway, always easing around each corner. Then he disappeared.

He didn't come back for a long time. Delia toyed with the idea of going to look for him, then decided she'd better not risk the sergeant's already tenuous goodwill.

"Stop! Police!"

Her heart raced as Griffin's cool, clear voice pierced the silence. Oh, God, he'd found someone. She gripped the door handle and held her breath, waiting for shots. But all she heard after that were voices, softer than before. Griffin's and another man's.

It didn't *sound* too dangerous. She crept closer, following Griffin's steps. When she peered around the corner, she saw him standing in the driveway, talking calmly with a burly, bearded man. As he talked, he shined the flashlight into the bushes behind the house.

"So what happened?" she asked as she brazenly approached the two men.

The bearded one jumped, then cursed. "Who's she?" he demanded suspiciously.

"No one you need to worry about," Griffin answered smoothly. "She's part of the Ride Along program."

"Never heard of it," the man said with a disapproving frown.

"No matter." Griffin reached into his shirt pocket, pulled out a card and handed it to the man. "If you have anything else to report, call me."

Delia said nothing else until she and Griffin were again cruising in the patrol car. "So what happened back there?" she asked. "Why did you yell 'Stop! Police!'?"

Griffin entered some mysterious code into the computer as he answered. "Mr. Hutchins came home shortly before I arrived and found his burglar alarm had been tripped. He was having a look around and we surprised each other, that's all."

"Did you draw your gun?" Her gaze drifted to the holster belt around his lean hips.

He rolled his eyes. "No. But don't worry. If this turns out to be a typical Saturday night, you'll get your fill of violence."

Delia winced. His accusation was too close to the truth for her to deny. She did want to be part of the action. Not that she would wish anyone to be hurt, but...ah, hell, she'd drive herself crazy if she thought too hard about why she was here. "Did someone break in?" she continued quietly.

"Apparently not. Someone might have tried, then gotten scared by the alarm."

The dispatcher's voice came over the radio; domestic disturbance on Cunningham. Griffin picked up the radio's handset and spoke into it briefly.

Delia's heart thudded in her chest. "We're going to a domestic disturbance?"

"Yes. And you *will* remain in the car this time."

Delia grappled with her temper for a moment, subdued it, then pondered the most effective way to voice her objections. "Sergeant Griffin," she finally said, "how am I going to learn about police work if you won't let me watch?"

"I can't have you getting in the way, confusing the issue," he said evenly. End of discussion.

It wasn't hard to spot the domestic disturbance once they reached Cunningham. Every resident on the block, it appeared, had turned out to watch the middle-aged couple screaming at each other in their front yard.

"Stay in the car," Griffin repeated as he jumped out.

For heaven's sake, if all these ordinary people could stand around watching, so could she. She surreptitiously exited the car and ambled up to the crowd until she was one of them.

"What's going on?" she asked a young woman standing next to her.

"The usual," the woman answered in a bored-sounding voice. "Joe is drunk, and Carmen won't let him in the house."

"This happen often?"

"'Bout once a week. They sure can kick up a fuss."

That was an understatement. Both combatants were waving their arms threateningly and screaming at the tops of their lungs, using a creative array of gestures and obscenities in English and Spanish.

"Do they ever hurt each other?"

"Nah, they just make a lot of noise."

Delia watched, fascinated and appalled at the same time. As a child, she had witnessed countless scenes just like this, when her father drank too much. She couldn't have been more than five, yet now she clearly remembered clinging to her mother's skirt, sobbing, pleading for them to stop screaming.

Griffin was attempting to talk to the couple, to get them to move into the house. He kept taking Joe by the elbow and trying to steer him toward the front porch. Joe kept jerking his arm out of Griffin's grasp.

"Now, come on, Mr. Domingo," Griffin coaxed. "I don't want to arrest you, but I'll have to if you don't calm down."

The threat of jail seemed to subdue him slightly. He appeared as if he might become halfway reasonable, but his wife was another matter.

"I don't want that drunken . . ." The tirade degenerated into Spanish. Then, "Not under my roof! He can sleep in the gutter for all I care, with all the other stinking drunks!"

Delia's college Spanish was rusty, but unless she missed her guess, Carmen had just called her husband a goat. Still, she could see something besides anger in the woman's flashing brown eyes—sorrow, perhaps, at seeing the man she loved in such a state. Then Delia saw something else that tore at her heart. Two children peered out the front door, one head above the other. They were scared to death.

She didn't think about what she did next, she simply reacted. Next thing she knew she was on the front porch behind Carmen, crouching so that she was on a level with the children, a boy and a girl. They raised their eyebrows in unison, but said nothing.

"Don't be frightened," she said in a low voice. "It's just a lot of yelling. It'll be over soon."

They continued to stare silently at her.

"Do you speak English?" she asked when it occurred to her that they might not understand.

The older one nodded cautiously. "'s my papa goin' to jail?"

"Well, maybe," Delia admitted. "But it might be the best—" Before she could finish her sentence, a strong hand gripped her arm and whirled her to her feet.

"What are you *doing?*" Tony demanded. If he'd been a wolf, he would have bared his fangs.

"Who *are* you?" Carmen asked suspiciously of Delia.

"I... The children..." she explained with a helpless shrug. "They were frightened, and..."

Carmen shot a guilty glance at the two moppets hovering in the open doorway. Then she returned her attention to her husband. "Now you see what you've done? You've frightened the children. You come in this house right now and apologize. Imagine how they must feel seeing their great big bear of a father ranting like a..." She again resorted to Spanish.

Joe now stood abjectly in the front yard, arms at his side, contemplating the toes of his cowboy boots. He looked up, gave his wife a watery, hopeful smile and meekly staggered to the front porch and inside the house. Carmen followed, slamming the door behind her.

Delia grinned, pleased with the outcome despite the fact that Griffin did not share her triumph. As the assembled onlookers began to wander away, the sergeant continued to stare at her with fire in his eyes.

Tony said not a word. He was afraid to—afraid that once he opened his mouth, he would explode and shake Delia Pryde until her pretty little teeth rattled.

"You don't seem pleased," she ventured when they'd driven a couple of blocks down the road.

Tony gritted his teeth. "If you *ever* pull a stunt like that again—"

"A stunt? What do you mean? I think I handled things pretty well."

"Yeah, right. 'The children...they were frightened,'" he said, mimicking her voice. "Give me a break!"

"Well it worked, didn't it? I didn't see you making much progress. All you wanted to do was throw the poor man in jail."

Unfortunately her tactics had worked better than his, Tony admitted to himself. That rankled him. He was a trained professional, and she was a...a bored, rich little socialite living out her fantasies playing Kojak.

"I wouldn't have arrested him unless it became absolutely necessary," he said. "But sometimes a small threat goes a long way toward cooling a guy off. Besides, I've dealt with the Domingos before. Eventually he would have—" Tony swore, loudly and colorfully. "That is not the point! The point is you just put your life in jeopardy and I will not stand for it."

"I did not put my life in jeopardy," she argued. "I checked first. One of the neighbors told me the Domingos' fights never get violent. There were no weapons involved. The situation was not dangerous."

"You have no idea what you're talking about. Domestic disturbances are unpredictable. Just a couple of months ago I answered a call very similar to this one. Suddenly the lady pulled a butcher knife out of her apron and stabbed her husband in the neck—right in front of me."

From the corner of his eye, he saw Delia grimace. "Did the husband die?" she asked.

"No. I managed to subdue the woman before she could get in a second lick. Sure was a lot of blood, though." He added this last comment with another sideways glance. He had to get through to his bouncy, overly cheerful little passenger. "For cryin' out loud, this is not a school field trip. Do you know how many violent crimes we've had so far this year on my beat? More than four hundred. It can happen anywhere, anytime, and I will *not* allow it to happen to a civilian riding in my car. Is that clear?"

"Is this personal, or would you react this way toward any Ride Along?"

Maybe it was a little personal, he conceded. He had been raised to protect women, especially small, soft, helpless-looking ones. He hadn't always succeeded. The possibility that he might fail again was enough to give him nightmares. "I don't approve of the Ride Along program," he finally said.

"Yes, I guess you'd resent any interloper riding in your squad car. You're a man's man and a cop's cop. You work alone and you like it that way. Am I right?"

Tony swore again and made an abrupt, and very illegal, U-turn in the middle of the street.

"What are you doing?"

"I'm taking you back to the station. They can bust me back to foot patrol, they can fire me, they can threaten me with red-hot coals, but I'm not letting you ride with me. You're going to get yourself killed. Worse, you're going to get me killed."

He expected an angry retort, but Delia slumped back into her seat without a word. Good, he'd finally managed to get through to her. Not that it mattered. He was going to dump her off as fast as he could and never see her again.

"Damn," he muttered, making another sharp turn and stamping on the gas pedal.

Delia sat up, instantly alert. "Now what?"

Tony grabbed for the radio. "This is Car 346, in pursuit of a blue Buick Skylark moving erratically, proceeding northeast on Metropolitan...." Even as he drove and talked, he was punching numbers into the computer.

The Skylark sped up and veered around a corner. So did Tony. He turned on his lights and siren.

"They're throwing stuff out the windows!" Delia shouted.

"Drugs," Tony said. "Damn, I knew that was the car." He grabbed for the radio again. "Car 346 in pursuit of stolen Skylark, turning south on Lybrand, now crossing—" he squinted out the window at the passing street sign "—Bedelia."

The blue car lurched over a median onto a side street. Tony followed. Another squad car joined the chase. The blue car turned into an alley. Dead end.

"Two suspects just got out of the car, fleeing on foot," Tony said hurriedly. "Backup's here. We're pursuing." As he opened his door, he turned to Delia. "Stay in the damn car this time or I'll handcuff you to the door!"

Two

Delia hunched down as two officers followed Griffin down the alley and over a fence. This time she had no intention of disobeying. She might be a little impulsive at times, but she wasn't a fool. Whoever had been driving that car was probably dealing drugs, and drug dealers were dangerous. That was one thing Uncle Tab had drilled into her head.

Uncle Tab... If he could see her now he would disown her.

Tab Shenniker was the man who had raised her from the age of seven, when her mother had died. Her father, who had left two years before, certainly would not have been in any condition to look after a child, even if he'd been inclined to. Delia had been destined for the foster-care system until her social worker had located Uncle Tab. He had been estranged from Delia's mother for years, hadn't ever even laid eyes on his niece, as a matter of fact. But as soon as he heard of her existence and her plight, he'd rushed to claim her, Delia's own Daddy Warbucks. From the moment he had scooped her into his arms and held her close against his big, brawny chest, Delia had been showered with love, security and all the material possessions she could have dreamed of. She'd never wanted for another thing.

Tab Shenniker was also a chief at Tony Griffin's station. Delia intended to keep that tidbit to herself.

Uncle Tab had been the one to plant the Ride Along idea in her head, although he hadn't realized it at the time. "You're not cut out for police work, Dee," he had told her a few weeks ago, when she'd first tested the waters by casually mentioning that she might look into joining the police force. "You have no idea what you'd be getting into. Think of the grisliest slasher movie you've ever seen—real crimes are ten times worse than that. I know you. You don't have the stomach for it. You wouldn't last ten minutes on the beats in my sector."

Well, she'd lasted more than ten minutes. But she hadn't seen anything gruesome yet.

Uncle Tab was right about one thing—she was a bit squeamish. But that was something she could overcome, she was sure. Her uncle had instilled in her a deep and abiding respect for police work. To play a part in getting criminals off the street—nothing could be more important.

She consulted her watch. The officers had disappeared almost ten minutes ago. What was taking so long? What if they never came back? The thought of Tony Griffin getting hurt made her stomach tighten painfully. She didn't know him well, and he certainly hadn't extended her much courtesy, but he was extraordinarily... alive. She couldn't bring herself to think of him any other way.

When almost fifteen minutes had crawled by, she heard voices from the alley behind her. "Oh, great," she muttered. Here she was, alone with three police cars in a dark alley.... She sighed with relief when she realized the voices belonged to the cops. One of them had a handcuffed man in tow. Good, they'd caught one of the suspects, at least, Delia thought with a surge of triumph. And there was Tony.... When had she started thinking of him as *Tony?*

He opened his car door. "You still here?

"Where did you expect me to be?"

He climbed in. "I half expected you to follow us over that fence."

"I wouldn't do anything that—" She gasped as her heart tried to force its way into her throat. "Tony! Uh, I mean, Sergeant Griffin, you've got blood all over you," she croaked as she grabbed his face in her hands and roughly turned his head back and forth, searching for the source of the dark stain on his cheek.

He ducked out of her grasp. "Cut it out, Delia. I'm not hurt." But he wasn't nearly as disgusted as he pretended. Her concern for his well-being touched something inside him. As for the effect of her soft hands on his skin...

He cocked the rearview mirror so he could examine his face, then rubbed at the stain with his index finger. "It's just mud. We had a scuffle in a parking lot."

She looked a little pale, Tony thought as he started the engine. Or maybe it was just the moonlight casting a pale glow on her fair skin. At any rate, she was much more subdued than she'd been. Maybe he could tolerate her after all.

The radio was quiet. Hopefully there would be a short respite before the bars closed at two. Then things would start hopping.

The other two cars pulled out of the way to let him out. His officers would take care of the arrest and wait for the evidence team to comb the Buick, which was fine with him. The chase had pumped him full of adrenaline. He wasn't in the mood to sit around and wait.

"I need to clean up. You want to stop and get some doughnuts or something?" he asked Delia.

"I thought you were taking me back to the station."

"Look, I'll make a deal with you. You can finish the shift with me. I'll even let you get out of the car on some of the calls, if it'll make you happy. But you have to keep your mouth shut and stay out of the way."

She was nodding enthusiastically. "I'll be good, I promise. No more interfering."

"And if I tell you to stay in the car—"

"I'll stay in the car and keep my head down."

"Good." Inexplicably, he felt better than he had in days. Maybe it was the fact that he'd finally nailed that stolen Skylark. The car had been described to him several times in connection with drug deals, and Tony had chased it and lost it twice this week. As a bonus, the suspect they'd caught was ready to name names.

Tony smiled at Delia. She wasn't so bad. "You like glazed or chocolate-covered?"

Delia was knocked speechless for a moment. That smile had transformed him from a brooding Heathcliff to a...well, there simply was no comparison. He was gorgeous, and the deviltry she saw in his dark eyes made her heart beat faster than the sixty-mile-per-hour car chase had.

"I like the filled kind, actually," she managed to say in a seminormal voice. "Raspberry. But I'll take what I can get."

Nothing more was said until they pulled into the parking lot of an all-night convenience store with a sign that read Go-Go Grocers. Then Tony asked, "Were you scared?"

"During the chase? No. I knew you were in control of the car all the while. When I thought I saw blood— now *that* scared me," she admitted, relieved to see her escort softening up a bit. She surveyed the shabby storefront. "This is where you get doughnuts?"

"Every night at 2.00 a.m., like clockwork," he answered as they got out of the car and went inside the store. He nodded toward a plump, neon-orange-haired woman who stood behind the small bakery case. "Evenin', Carmeline. Pick me out a couple of fresh bearclaws." To Delia, he said, "Get whatever you want for yourself. I'm going to the washroom."

Delia made her selections while the bored-looking Carmeline pulled the pastries haphazardly out of the glass case and dropped them into a sack.

"Are any of these raspberry?" Delia asked.

"Hell if I know," the clerk replied with a roll of her eyes.

When Tony reappeared, he was once again impeccably groomed. He paid for the doughnuts, and Carmeline sniffed loudly in obvious disdain as she handed over the change.

"I don't think she's too fond of you," Delia whispered as they made their way back to the squad car. "Why do you keep coming here?"

"Carmeline? Oh, she's just mad at me, and it's understandable. This store's been hit twice in the past three weeks," Tony explained. "I think she blames the cops for not doing a better job catching the robbers. But she does sell the best doughnuts in South Dallas."

The reminder of this neighborhood's constant violence made Delia shiver. But all she had to do was glance at Tony and she felt safe. He might resent her presence, but he would protect her.

They sat in the squad car and indulged in pastries for a few minutes without talking. The filled doughnut Delia ate was cherry, not raspberry, but it still wasn't bad. "Mmm, I didn't realize how hungry I was."

"Adrenaline does that to you," Tony said.

"Is that why cops like doughnut shops?" she asked as seriously as she dared.

He shrugged, taking her teasing in stride. "This cop, anyway. Whenever I get a rush like I got chasing that guy, nothing will do but a heavy influx of refined sugar to my system. But every cop is different. Franklin gets a craving for fried chicken about three o'clock in the morning. O'Dell has a thing for Slurpees. Rashim just chews bubble gum all night."

"I'll fit right in, then," she said cheerfully. "Chocolate ice cream's what I get a yen for."

He gave her a penetrating stare, the kind that could freeze a waterfall, effectively canceling the brief camaraderie they'd shared. "What do you mean, you'll fit right in?"

She hadn't actually planned to confess. But she was so excited about her plans for the future that the answer to Tony's question came spilling out. "I've applied to the police department. I've already had my interview, taken all the tests—"

"Applied as *what?*"

"A police officer, of course."

"You're kidding, I hope."

Delia bit her lip to prevent an emotional outburst as she wrapped the remainder of her jelly doughnut in a napkin and dropped it back into the empty sack. She wasn't hungry anymore. Her uncle hadn't taken her announcement seriously, either. Everyone assumed that because she was small-boned, passably pretty and financially comfortable, she wasn't fit to do anything strenuous, unpleasant or the least bit dangerous.

Maybe she wasn't accustomed to the grittier aspects of life. Even as a child, living in one of the scariest neighborhoods in Chicago, her mother had managed to shield her from the worst of the ugliness that surrounded them. But that didn't mean Delia was incapable of educating herself.

"You aren't kidding?" Tony asked when she didn't respond.

"I am perfectly serious. You have something against women in law enforcement?"

"Hell, no. The best partner I ever had was a woman. But she was..." He gestured with his hands to indicate what Delia guessed was a goodly sized female. "And you're..." His hands dropped and he shrugged helplessly. "You'll never make it through training. I'll be surprised if they even accept you."

"Well, thank you for that vote of confidence," she said sharply as she used a paper napkin to wipe a dab of red goo off her chin. "For your information, I've already passed all the entrance exams, *including* physical fitness and strength." Barely, but she didn't admit that.

Tony issued a skeptical-sounding *hmph*. "Do you know the first thing an officer has to learn? To follow orders. And you do that about as well as . . . as well as you wipe cherry filling off your face."

"What?"

He picked up another napkin. "You missed some," he said as he leaned over and gently dabbed at a spot on Delia's cheek.

The gesture was so unconsciously intimate that Delia went as gooey inside as the doughnut she'd just discarded. Suddenly the car's interior was too small, too warm. She could almost hear the hiss and crackle of electricity. Their eyes met and held, and she knew he felt the same zing of awareness.

She still wanted to throttle the man for his pig-headed refusal to look beyond her outward appearance. But for some unknown reason—something in his dark brown eyes, perhaps—she also wanted him to hold her in his arms. It made no sense, but since when were hormones sensible?

The napkin disappeared, replaced by the warmth of Tony's fingers against her cheek. Delia's gaze dropped to his incredibly sexy mouth. Was he actually going to kiss her? Here, in a parking lot lit up like daytime, where anybody passing by could see? Part of her prayed that he would, but the saner half of her brain told her to pull back. The chemistry was there, but the timing was disastrous.

The radio hissed and the dispatcher's tension-edged voice filled the car. "We have a shooting reported at

1214 Brumly, Apartment 2. Any officer in the vicinity please respond.''

Tony blinked as he careened back to reality. His hand dropped along with his gaze. "That's me," he said as he grabbed for the radio. "Three-forty-six responding to that shooting. I'm about five blocks away." He switched on the siren and the lights as he screeched out of the parking lot.

"Shooting?" Delia squeaked.

Tony nodded grimly, his mind already gearing up for the scene that awaited him. Later he would think about what almost happened back there.

It took less than three minutes to reach the address on Brumly, a decrepit apartment building with a weedy front lawn and several windows broken. Tony pulled the car onto the curb and jumped out.

Halfway across the yard he looked over his shoulder, saw Delia trailing along behind him and hesitated. Did the infuriating woman not have a shred of self-preservation instinct? Dammit, he didn't have time to deal with her right now! But before he could decide what to do about her, a shrill wail of distress claimed his attention.

"They shot my brother!" A woman wearing a faded, flowered housedress and a head full of curlers barrelled out the building's front entrance.

"Are they still here?" Tony demanded curtly.

"No, they ran off just before you drove up," she said pointing down the street. "Help my brother, please!"

Tony brushed past the woman and went inside.

"Down the hall and to the right," the woman said as she followed.

As he strode down the hall, Tony knew in the back of his mind that he should have made Delia stay in the car. But hell, if the shooters were gone there was probably no danger. He'd let her get a good, hard look at whatever awaited them. Hopefully, afterward she wouldn't want to set foot out of the patrol car for the rest of the night.

The door to Apartment 2 was open. The smell of gunpowder still hung in the air, along with another smell—death. Tony knew immediately that the young man he found sprawled on the floor was beyond help.

The woman knew it, too. Tony could see it in her face, in the hollowness of her eyes. "Did you see what kind of car they were in?" he asked tersely.

"Uh . . . black truck, shiny new," she replied in a dreamlike voice. "One of them all-terrain jeep-looking things."

He could hear the arrival of another squad car. His officers could secure the crime scene. He was going after the guys who did this.

"Don't touch anything," he barked at the woman as he turned. That's when he saw Delia, standing in the doorway, her eyes transfixed on the carnage, her face as green as pea soup.

Damn, this was exactly what he had feared would happen. He grabbed her by her slender shoulders and jerked her away from the door. "Go back to the car," he ordered as he propelled her down the hall. His concern for her warred with the urgency he felt to chase down the scum who were getting away.

"I could help," she said weakly. "That poor woman—"

The woman in question was wailing again.

"You aren't going to help anyone by passing out or throwing up. Please, just this once, do as I—" His back was toward a shadowy hallway. He realized his mistake too late. He whirled around just as a rush of air announced the impending assault. The butt of a shotgun smacked him square in the forehead. Delia screamed. That was the last thing he heard.

Delia watched in horror as Tony crumpled at her feet and the gunman lunged past her. He didn't get far. At the building's front door, he was met by two officers who quickly and efficiently disarmed him and threw him to the ground.

"What happened?" one of the officers demanded.

Delia somehow pulled her wits together. "He came out of the shadows and hit Sergeant Griffin in the head with the end of his gun," she said. Then she pointed down the hall. "There's a dead man down there. According to the woman, a couple of other guys got away in a black truck."

The officers went into action. One continued down the hall while the other tended to Tony. A good-sized goose egg was forming on his forehead, and his right arm was twisted awkwardly beneath him.

"Jeez, he's out cold," said the officer, a tall, good-looking redhead whose name badge identified him as S. Reilly. He checked Tony's pulse and his breathing, then lifted one of his eyelids and shined his flashlight into the eye. "Ambulance should be here soon."

Please let him be all right, Delia prayed as she knelt beside Tony and allowed her fingers to stroke the side of his strong, tanned face. He might be a stubborn, close-minded tough guy, but he certainly didn't deserve this.

Another siren howled up the street. Within seconds the paramedics arrived, along with more uniforms and what Delia guessed to be homicide detectives.

"Body's in there," one of the officers said to the plainclothesmen. To the paramedics he said, "Help Sergeant Griffin."

Delia scuttled out of the way as the stretcher was brought in and Tony's inert form was placed on it. "He was hit in the forehead," she said, hovering close by.

"Who are you?" one of the paramedics asked her.

"A...a friend. Can I go along?"

"Sorry, not unless you're a relative or a police officer."

She briefly considered posing as a detective, when another inspiration struck. "I'm Chief Shenniker's niece," she said, dropping names for the first time that night.

The paramedics were unimpressed.

"You gotta stay here anyway," said Reilly. "You're a witness. We'll want to get your statement."

This was the last place she wanted to stay. But apparently she didn't have any choice. She followed the stretcher as far as the ambulance.

Just before he was put aboard, Tony opened his eyes and stared directly at Delia. His face lit up with a brief but beatific smile. "Hey, gorgeous, how's about a date?" he said with more strength than she would have thought possible.

She was both relieved that he was conscious and embarrassed at the personal nature of his outburst, which had caused Reilly and the paramedics to snicker. "Soon as you're up and around, handsome, we'll talk about it," she called to him in the same vein,

but she doubted he heard her. His eyes had closed
again.

"You think he'll be okay?" she asked Reilly anx-
iously.

The officer nodded, though his expression was
guarded. "The sarge is tough."

Delia sat on the stoop of the apartment building,
waiting an interminable amount of time. She'd wanted
to observe the detectives, the evidence team and the
coroner in action, but even if they'd been willing to let
her in the apartment to watch—which they hadn't—
she wasn't sure her stomach could have survived. So
she sat outside in the crisp, late-night autumn and let
her mind go numb.

When the detectives finally got around to inter-
viewing her, their questions were endless and tedious,
especially since all she wanted to do was get out of
there and check on Tony.

"Yes, Sergeant Griffin and I were the first to ar-
rive," she answered for the third time. "Yes, the sister pointed that way and said the men who shot her
brother had just fled down the street.... Yes, I saw the
man come out of the shadows and hit Sergeant Griffin with the butt of his gun... Of course I can identify him, but for heaven's sake, he ran right into two
policemen. Is his identity in question?"

It was, the detective informed her curtly. Apparently he didn't appreciate her impertinence. She was
the only witness to the actual assault, he told her, so
they would probably want her to pick the man out of
a photo lineup.

Terrific. Now there was no possible way to keep
Uncle Tab from finding out about this. He would have

kittens when he discovered she'd gone on patrol in the roughest neighborhood in town. He thought the Ride Along program was a fine idea—as long as it wasn't his niece riding along.

By the time the police completed their questioning, it was four in the morning. Officer Reilly offered to drive Delia back to the station to pick up her car.

"I checked with the hospital," he told her once they were alone. "The sarge is gonna be okay. He's got a broken wrist and a concussion, and they're keeping him overnight for observation, but he's fine."

Delia knew she should have felt relief that his injuries were minor. But the thought of that vibrantly alive man lying in a hospital bed, undoubtedly in pain, filled her with anxiety.

She recalled the invitation he'd issued just before going to the hospital, and smiled. He'd obviously been knocked senseless at that point. The last person he'd want to take out on a date was her, after the trouble she'd caused him. More than likely, as soon as his wits returned, he'd curse her up one side and down another.

"Are you really the chief's niece?" Reilly asked.

"Yeah." And right now she wished she were anybody else.

He gave a low whistle. "He's gonna nail the sarge's hide to the wall and use it for target practice when he finds out about this."

"Oh, this incident certainly wasn't Sergeant Griffin's fault," Delia said emphatically. "He didn't want me there in the first place, and he tried his best to keep me out of danger. I didn't listen to him. I'm afraid his injuries are all my fault. I distracted him." It was the first time she had admitted this, even to herself.

"If I'd just stayed in the car like he wanted me to... if I hadn't gotten sick when I saw that poor man... if I hadn't argued with Tony, distracting him, he might have been more alert to the gunman's presence...."

"Don't blame yourself," Reilly said with a fatalistic shrug. "It could have been worse."

When Delia realized with crushing clarity just how bad it could have been, her eyes filled with tears. With her misplaced bravado, she had done Tony Griffin a grave disservice. She would make it up to him if it was the last thing she did.

Three

———

Tony knew it was morning, but that didn't mean he wanted to open his eyes. He could feel an obnoxiously cheery burst of sunlight warming his face, which would only make his headache that much worse.

So he kept his eyes closed. But a subtly pleasant scent—something vaguely familiar, intriguingly feminine, kept teasing his nostrils until he was forced to satisfy his curiosity. He cracked open first one eye, then the other—just enough so that he could peer through his lashes.

Delia Pryde. She was sitting by his bed, an anxious angel of mercy, he mused dreamily, still not quite awake.

"Where'd you get hair that color?" he asked in a scratchy voice.

She jumped. "Oh, Tony... ah, Sergeant Griffin, you're awake." She smiled, obviously pleased. "The nurses said you had a rough night, with the headache and all, so they let you sleep this morning. It's almost ten o'clock. Do you want breakfast?"

Headache. That was an understatement. It felt like someone with an Uzi was using the inside of his skull for target practice.

Oddly, the realization that he was in the hospital didn't worry him, or even surprise him very much. He knew he wasn't dying, and he also knew there was a good reason for him to be here. He just couldn't quite recall what it was.

"I'd love breakfast," he said, trying to clear his mind of the fog. "Bagels and cream cheese and ham and eggs and freshly squeezed orange juice," he said, knowing his chances of getting anything remotely like that were minimal. "But first... how did I get here?"

Delia's crystalline eyes widened. "Oh, dear, you don't remember?"

"I remember responding to a call about a shooting...." His left hand wandered up to gingerly test the sore spot on his forehead. Ah, yes, now it was coming back: the eerie itch at the back of his neck that meant someone was watching him, the realization that he'd put himself in a vulnerable position, the reflexes, fast but not fast enough to ward off the attack. He also recalled a confused muddle of emotions ranging from anger and frustration to fear for Delia's safety.

Obviously his fear had been unwarranted, because she looked about as whole and healthy as a female could get. So his anger won out. He narrowed his eyes as he pondered what scathing thing he wanted to say to her first.

"Oh, dear, you do remember," she said, then murmured, "might have been better for me if you hadn't."

"What are you doing here, anyway?" he demanded.

"I was worried about you."

"Spare me. As you can see, I'm f-fine..." His words trailed off when he noticed his right arm. "What's this thing around my arm?"

"It's a cast. You broke your wrist."

"Oh, for cryin' out—that's great. That's just marvelous."

"At least you weren't seriously injured," she pointed out.

"That's easy for you to say. You don't have to contemplate some boring desk job for the next three months. And I probably wouldn't have been injured at all if it hadn't been for you."

Delia tensed as if anticipating a blow. She studied her sneakers and tugged at her lower lip with her front teeth. "I know," she said softly.

Well, at least he didn't have to argue that point. "Could I have some water?" he asked. A pitcher and a cup sat on a counter just out of his reach. He could have gotten up to get it, he supposed. There was nothing wrong with his legs. But just the thought of lifting his head off the pillow made him want to groan.

"Sure." Delia hopped out of her chair and reached for the pitcher, once again in her angel-of-mercy mode. She seemed happy to be doing something.

He accepted the cup she'd poured, raised his head just enough to get the straw in his mouth and took a couple of swallows. When he handed her back the cup, their fingers brushed. If she noticed, she gave no indication. But the split-second contact was enough to remind Tony of how her hands felt on his skin—soft, warm and stronger than they looked.

"What else can I get you?" she asked brightly.

"Why are you so damn cheerful all the time?"

She wilted like a delicate rose pelted by raindrops. "Hospital patients usually like to be cheered up. But for you, I'll try to be more glum, if it'll make you feel better."

"What would make me feel better is for you to leave me alone and let me suffer in peace," he said. The incessant pounding in his head was making his tongue even sharper than usual. But he hadn't wanted to deal with Delia last night when he was in full control of his faculties, and he surely wasn't in the mood to deal with her now. If she knew what was good for her she'd scoot along out of his life. If she insisted on hanging around, he was either going to wring her slender little neck or... or take her to bed.

In the instant it had taken him to visualize her beneath him, gloriously naked, his blood had surged and an uncomfortable tightness had taken up residence in his loins. He shifted his blankets slightly, realizing as he did that he was wearing one of those stupid hospital gowns with no back. He was practically naked himself, and already in bed.

He glanced at the bed next to him, where an elderly man slept. Too bad this wasn't a private room, Tony mused.

"What are you smiling about?"

Had he been smiling? How could he smile through this headache? He couldn't come up with an acceptable explanation for his amusement, however, so he ignored the question. "Where're my clothes?"

"Your uniform's in the closet. Your gun is in a safe somewhere—you can get it when you check out."

"Any idea when that'll be?"

"They're going to release you in a little while," she said, sitting in her chair with her hands folded primly in her lap. "Is there someone you can stay with for a couple of days? You shouldn't be alone, not with that concussion. You could slip into a coma and no one would ever know."

"First you're cheerful, now you're morbid," he mumbled.

"Is there someone you can stay with?" she persisted.

"No, but I'll manage."

"So, Officer Reilly was right. No family around to take care of you?"

"Nope. They all live in Michigan."

"A girlfriend?"

He almost smiled again, catching himself just in time. He could have sworn Delia sounded a little more anxious when she posed that question than when she'd asked the others. "No girlfriend," he said. And he'd be damned if he'd impose on any of his buddies, not while he was in this condition. That would be downright embarrassing. "I'll manage," he said again.

"How? With that arm in a cast you won't even be able to open a can of soup by yourself."

"So I'll order out for pizza."

"Every meal? Stubborn man, you would starve to death before asking someone for help."

Oh, so that was her angle. "I've had all the help from you I can take, thank you. Any further assistance might kill me."

She visibly flinched this time, and he regretted his careless, caustic words. But at least she understood now why he'd wanted her to stay in the car, and why he hated the Ride Along program. Just as he had predicted, she'd distracted him from his duties. They were both lucky the outcome hadn't been any more serious than a bump on the head and a busted wrist.

"Did they catch the guy?" he asked her.

She brightened. "Yes, they did. I'm going to meet with the detective later today to identify the suspect in a photo lineup."

Tony was glad the scumbag had been caught, but he was uncomfortable with the idea of Delia's involvement. As a Ride Along she was supposed to be an impartial observer, not a participant. "I could identify him," he said. "I only saw him for a second, but I remember exactly what he looked like."

"Nonsense. You're not in any shape to go anywhere except home and straight to bed. Anyway, there's nothing dangerous about this. Officer Reilly assured me the man won't know who made the ID."

"He'll know later, if this goes to court," Tony pointed out. "The D.A. will probably call you in as a witness. No, I don't like it. Tell 'em you won't do it."

"Of course I'll do it. Officer Reilly said I was the only one who witnessed the assault."

"The assault's not important. The murder's important."

"He might not have done the shooting," Delia said, shivering. "The victim's sister doesn't think he's the one. So if I don't identify him, he might get out. I won't let that happen."

There was a certain cold conviction in her voice when she spoke that kept Tony from arguing further.

He knew he wouldn't win. One thing he could say without hesitation about Delia Pryde: she was stubborn. She also appeared to have a tough conscience.

"So, it looks like you'll need a ride home," she said, changing the subject.

"I'll call a cab."

"I can take you. You don't live too far from me."

"Oh? And how do you know that?"

"Officer Reilly said—"

"Please, that's enough about Officer Reilly." Sean Reilly. The tall, redheaded man had an eye for the ladies. Naturally he would home in on Delia the moment she was alone. "I hope that Irish Casanova didn't make a nuisance of himself."

Delia looked faintly amused. "Don't be preposterous. He was a perfect gentleman. *He* didn't try to kiss me over doughnuts."

Tony could feel the blood rushing to his face. He'd pushed that uncomfortable moment aside, when he'd touched Delia's cheek and looked into those clear, clear blue eyes and thought about things he shouldn't have. Now it came rushing back.

"And Officer Reilly didn't ask me out on a date," Delia added with a mischievous smirk.

"I never did that!"

"Oh, yes, you did. I have at least three witnesses, including the paramedics who were loading you into the ambulance at the time. You opened your eyes and shouted out for all the world to hear, 'Hey, gorgeous, how's about a date?' "

Tony covered his face with his one good hand. He supposed he should thank his lucky stars he hadn't yelled out something like "Hey, hot stuff, why don't you rub baby oil all over my naked body?" Or worse.

"What did you answer?" he asked.

Now it was her turn to be embarrassed. "I didn't dignify the question with an answer," she said. "You were obviously delirious."

She was lying. He could tell by the way she avoided his gaze.

"I mean, you've made it perfectly clear I'm the last person you want to spend an evening with. Right?"

Oh, if she only knew.

Delia turned her white Mazda Miata onto Vickery, as Tony directed. Somehow she had managed to convince him to let her drive him home from the hospital. Part of the reason she'd wanted to, aside from a genuine desire to be of service, was a curiosity about what sort of house or apartment he might live in.

She had always loved this lower Greenville neighborhood, with its tree-lined streets and charming older homes. A little less grand than the neighborhood she'd grown up in, this area had nonetheless come into its own over the past few years. Property values had skyrocketed as the yuppies had taken over.

"It's the fourth house on the right, the gray one with the black shutters," Tony said.

"Oh, what a pretty house," Delia exclaimed as she turned into the drive.

"You sound surprised. Did you think I'd live in a dump?"

"No, of course not. I just said it was pretty, that's all." But she was a bit surprised to find this quaint little two-story Queen Anne, with its steeply pitched roof and a walkway lined with bright-leaved colea, belonged to Sergeant Griffin. She had expected something more modern, something sleek and functional.

"It used to be my great-aunt's," Tony explained as they approached the bright red front door. "She died and the house went to my father, who had no use for it. But I was looking for a change. I was ready to leave those Michigan winters behind. So I bought the house from Dad, sight unseen. . . . Did I invite you in?"

"No, but I'm coming in anyway. Look, I just want to get you settled in, make sure you have enough food in the pantry for a couple of days—that kind of thing," she said when she thought he might challenge her. "Were you pleased when you saw the house for the first time?"

"Not exactly. It was definitely a little old lady's house, right down to the pink carpets and the poodle wallpaper. But I've been working on it. And it's not necessary for you to 'settle' me in. I'll be fine."

He said this while opening the door. Delia followed him inside whether he liked it or not.

She took a quick look around, and felt vindicated. *This* looked like Tony Griffin. The wood floors had been stripped of their pink carpets, then finished to a high gloss. The walls were white, the furniture starkly modern in shades of gray and black. Skylights had been added, but on the back side of the house so as not to compromise its appearance from the street.

"You've done a wonderful job," she said. A colorful rug and some bright throw pillows might have softened the decor's severity, but she refrained from making any suggestions. "Now go get into bed. I'll fix you something to eat before I leave. You didn't touch your breakfast at the hospital."

"By the time that doctor finished poking and prodding me, it was stone-cold. Come on, Delia, you don't have to stay. You've done your..." He closed his eyes and reached for the door frame to steady himself.

"Sergeant Griffin!" Instinctively she reached out to support him, grabbing his upper arm.

"It's just a little dizzy spell," he said patiently. "No reason to be alarmed."

"I'm not alarmed," she said stiffly. "But I want you to go to bed this instant, before you fall and break something else." Still holding his firmly muscled arm, she more or less dragged him toward the stairs.

"Were you perhaps my third-grade teacher in a former life?" he asked. "Mrs. Wiggins used to drag me around by my arm like this." Still, he went along with Delia. If he had wanted to balk, she knew, her puny strength would be no match for his brawn.

She didn't feel the slightest bit like a prim schoolteacher. In fact, the strongly muscled bicep against the palm of her hand had her thinking about things she shouldn't—like what the rest of him would feel like to her touch. Was his chest as hard as she imagined beneath that bulletproof vest he wore? Was that flat stomach rippled with muscles?

"That's the linen closet," Tony said as she reached for a random doorknob once they reached the top of the stairs. He was obviously amused.

"Well, where's your bedroom?" And my, didn't that sound intimate. She hoped her face wasn't turning as pink as it felt.

"To the left," he said softly.

She was almost relieved to see that his room wasn't as immaculate as the rest of the house. The dresser was littered with comfortable male clutter, and there were a few items of clothing draped here and there on doorknobs and over the backs of chairs. The Danish-style furniture, too, was comforting—still sleek and modern, but the warm wood tones were a welcome departure from gray and black.

The hastily made bed, though, sported linens with gray, black and white stripes. Tony obviously had taste, but he was in a monochrome rut.

Her gaze remained riveted to the bed as Tony, using only his good hand, removed his holster with some difficulty and carefully locked his gun in the drawer of his bedside table. The Technicolor bruise on his forehead made her wince. She felt a strong urge to help him undress, to gently lay him down on that comfortable-looking bed and soothe his pain.

He sat down on the edge of the mattress to remove his shoes. "You look like you could use a nap yourself," he said. "How late did they keep you up last night?"

"I managed to grab a couple of hours' sleep this morning," she fibbed.

"You should have stayed in bed instead of rushing to the hospital."

"I wanted to see for myself that you were okay." And besides, she couldn't bring herself to close her eyes. Every time she did, she saw that poor dead man sprawled on the carpet and smelled the gunpowder all over again. She wasn't sure if she would ever get another restful night's sleep.

"I'll be fine," he repeated as he unbuttoned his shirt and unzipped the bulky vest, revealing a thin, snowy-white undershirt. "Go home and get some rest."

Something warm uncoiled in Delia's stomach as he pulled off the shirt. Where before she'd wanted to soothe him into that bed and nurture him, now all she could think about was joining him there and cuddling up next to that gorgeous chest and letting those strong arms enfold her.

When he reached for his pants, she whirled around and made for the door. Either he was very unself-conscious or he'd caught her staring and was deliberately trying to embarrass her. Since she was so painfully transparent, she suspected the latter.

"I'll go find you something to eat," she mumbled as she made a hasty exit.

He made a reply that she didn't quite catch. She stopped. "I'm sorry, what did you say?"

"I said could you bring me an ice pack, and maybe some aspirin? My head's killing me."

"I'll get them right away," she said before scuttling down the stairs.

Delia felt so guilty she wanted to kick herself. The man was injured. How could she stoop to having lascivious thoughts about him? And he must be feeling wretched to resort to asking her, or anyone, for anything. He seemed like the independent type to her, a man who hated to lean on anyone for the smallest favor.

As soon as Delia had left the room, Tony stripped down to his briefs and climbed into bed. He despised the idea of being incapacitated, even briefly, but Delia was right. He wasn't in any shape to take care of himself. His head pounded, his right arm throbbed all the way to his shoulder, he was hungry and he couldn't stand up for long enough to fix himself something to eat.

He eased his head back on the pillow and closed his eyes. Immediately, Delia's image, bright as a new copper penny, popped into his mind. If someone had to nurse him for a few hours, she would be his first choice. Aside from the fact she was beautiful, she had a comforting voice, sweet as a summer breeze, and a soothing touch.

Perhaps a bit *too* soothing. There was something about her skin against his...

She tapped on the door. "Sergeant Griffin? I have your ice pack and your aspirin."

"Come in. And Delia, you can call me Tony."

As she handed him two white tablets and a glass of water, her expression was guarded. "Oh? I thought you'd frown on such...intimacy."

If she'd purposely chosen that word to make him uncomfortable, she'd succeeded. *Intimacy* called to mind a lot more than first names. "Last night I did a lot of frowning," he said. "But I think under the circumstances, 'Sergeant Griffin' is a bit formal. You are in my bedroom, after all."

"And you're in no shape to do anything about it," she quipped. "Take your aspirin. And here's the ice pack."

She'd fashioned it from a plastic bag and a dish towel, Tony noted. "Very resourceful," he said as he examined her handiwork. He leaned back and settled the bag of ice cubes against his forehead. "Ah, that feels nice."

"What would you like to eat?" Delia asked. "Your refrigerator and pantry seem pretty well stocked."

"You don't have to cook—" he started to say, but she overrode his objection.

"I want to," she said, softly but insistently. "I have some time to kill before I go downtown anyway."

Tony could see that he wouldn't be able to dissuade her. She was intent on playing Florence Nightingale, and nothing would stand in her way. He had to admit, a small part of him enjoyed her attentiveness. He had lived alone for thirteen years, since he'd moved down here after graduating from college, and he'd forgotten how nice it was to have a woman close by. She looked so pretty and soft in her pale yellow designer sweat suit, and she smelled even better.

"Well, if you're determined to prepare a meal, how about bagels and cream cheese and ham and eggs and freshly squeezed orange juice?"

"That's the same breakfast you asked for in the hospital."

"And I'm still craving it."

"Do you have all those things in your kitchen?"

He shrugged. "Maybe."

"Well, I'll see what I can do," she said briskly as she turned to leave.

He started to call her back. He didn't really want her to fix him all that food. But he wondered just how far she would go. How much guilt did she harbor about her part in last night's drama?

He had his answer a short while later when she reappeared with a heavily laden tray, bearing everything he'd asked for and more: she'd added jelly for his bagel, a glass of milk in addition to the orange juice, the morning paper and even a red rose—plucked from his neighbor's bush, no doubt.

"Good Lord, Delia, you didn't have to go to this much trouble."

"I don't mind. I used to like to fix my uncle a big breakfast like this on Sunday mornings. That was before his doctor told him to lower his cholesterol." She sighed.

"Your uncle?"

"He raised me," she said with a fond smile. "My parents were divorced when I was little, and then my mother died. My father wasn't in any position to take care of me, so Uncle—my uncle took me in."

"Must have worked out okay. Do you still live with him?"

She frowned. "Of course not. I'm twenty-five, and I've been on my own for quite some time."

"Mmm, I thought you were younger. This is good, by the way," he said, nodding toward the omelet.

"Thank you," she said primly.

"So what do you do when you're not harassing police officers?" he asked.

She ignored the gibe. "I'm not really doing anything. I just finished a master's program at SMU, and I'm taking a well-deserved break." She glanced at her watch. "Oh, dear, I really have to go. Will you be all right?"

"I keep telling you, I'll be fine." Her ministrations should have been annoying. Instead, Tony was rather enjoying all the attention. Too bad it was guilt prompting Delia to hover, rather than any real fondness.

"I'll check back when I'm finished downtown."

"That's not necessary," he said with less-than-thorough conviction.

"Yes it is," she said firmly as she moved to take her leave. "Just leave the tray on the floor when you're done. I'll take care of it later."

"Delia . . ."

"Look, Tony. You might be bigger than me, but right now you're weak as a kitten and in no position to argue. I fully intend to take care of things for you until you're back on your feet."

This was too much. This pint-sized butterfly of a woman was trying to bully him! All right, as long as she was so determined to take care of him, he would make the job worthwhile.

"That's awful nice of you," he said with an evil smile. "Come to think of it, there are a lot of things to be done that I can't do while I'm laid up. The plants outside need watering, and I ought to pay some bills. No way can I write out checks with this cast on my arm. Oh, and there's a big pile of laundry in the utility room I've been meaning to get to. That could be a problem...."

"Exactly," she agreed. "You see? You do need some help. I'll be back shortly and I'll take care of everything."

After she was gone, Tony pursed his lips. He'd thought the mention of the laundry would dissuade her. Surely when she actually saw the formidable pile of dirty clothes... Hmm, what other tasks could he think up for her? Maybe he could ask her to wax the floors or mow the grass.

Yeah, that would do it, he decided, nodding with satisfaction. If she didn't run screaming from the house by nightfall, he would eat his cast.

Four

Delia's eyelids were drooping by the time she drove away from the downtown station later that afternoon. Picking out the gun-toting thug from the photo lineup had been a breeze, and the previously snarling detective had been pleased with her swift, positive ID. But the satisfaction of doing her civic duty couldn't compensate for Delia's lack of sleep. Not even the picture-perfect weather—warm and sunny, but with a light fall nip in the wind—could lift her spirits very high.

She toyed with the idea of stopping at home and crawling into bed for a couple of hours, then quickly discarded it. She wasn't quite ready to allow her mind to go idle. Sooner or later she would have to deal with that nightmarish murder scene and put it in the proper perspective, but she didn't think she could do it just yet. She would go straight back to Tony's instead.

She smiled then, amazed that she actually looked forward to playing nursemaid for the surly-but-sexy sergeant. Even the thought of his laundry didn't daunt her. He intended to take advantage of her offer of service—that wicked smile he'd flashed right before she left had told her that much. But right now she didn't care. She still felt enormously guilty for what she'd done to him, and it would take a lot of atonement before she could call it even.

Standing on his front porch a few minutes later, she hesitated before ringing the doorbell. She hated to get him out of bed, but earlier she'd locked the door behind her. Well, no help for it now. She pushed the button.

It took a while, but the door finally opened—slowly.

"Hi, it's just me, Delia," she said. "Sorry I dragged you out of b-b-b..." And she was lucky to get that much out, once she laid eyes on Tony. He stood in the doorway wearing a pair of faded jeans, snug in all the right places—and nothing more. Her gaze glued itself to his bronzed chest, to the dark mat of hair that formed a diamond then arrowed down his flat, corrugated belly to disappear beneath the waistband of his jeans.

Didn't the man own a robe?

Earlier she'd been plenty aware of his impressive physical assets, but she hadn't been prepared for a second look so soon. Her body reacted with a will of its own as tendrils of heat curled into her every fiber. It was all she could do not to touch him, to test the firmness of that chest with the palm of her hand.

"Come on in," he said, sounding neither pleased nor irritated to see her again. If he was aware of the fire he'd ignited inside of her, she couldn't tell. "You didn't drag me out of bed. I was watching the Cow-boys-Packers game."

"Oh? You must be feeling better, then."

He shrugged one muscular shoulder as she stepped inside.

"Who's winning?" she asked, more to make friendly conversation than out of curiosity.

"Packers, ten to seven. But it's only halftime."

She followed him into the living room. There, a blanket and a couple of bed pillows were strewn across the black leather couch. A television, previously hidden from sight inside a black enamel entertainment center, blared out a series of halftime scores from around the country.

Tony reached for the remote control and turned down the volume. "You can join me if you want."

"Ah, no, I don't think so," she quickly replied. Sit next to him among the blanket and pillows when he was half-naked? She was no dummy. "I'm not much of a football fan, I'm afraid."

"That's un-American," he said as he eased his six-foot frame onto the couch. "Not only that, it's un-Texan."

Delia watched in fascination as the muscles of his shoulders and back bunched and rippled in interesting combinations. "But I'm not a native Texan," she objected, pleased that she could carry on a coherent conversation while her heart was dancing around like a water droplet on a hot griddle. She had never experienced such a strong physical reaction to any man.

"So's half the Texas population, including me," he said. "Where're you from?"

"Chicago, not so far from your own home state of Michigan." But the last thing she wanted to discuss was her unsavory childhood. She didn't care to relive any of the unsettling memories that had been battering at her consciousness ever since last night's events had stirred them up. "I'll just get started on that laundry."

"Oh, right. Through the kitchen and to the left. Hey, do you think you could bring me a beer?"

"You shouldn't drink with that concussion," she objected.

He rolled his eyes. "Anything cold, then."

"Coming up." Relieved to be doing something constructive, she fetched a cold drink from the refrigerator. Tony's dark brown gaze never left the TV screen as she set the can on the glass coffee table in front of him. She left him to his football and went in search of laundry.

"Oh, my," she said aloud when she saw the mountain of dirty clothes. "What's he doing, saving it for a rainy day?" Just the same, she jumped right into the task with vigor. It was the least she could do. After she put the first load in, she headed outside to water the thirsty hanging baskets of plants that surrounded a small redwood hot tub on Tony's patio.

She lifted one edge of the hot tub cover and tested the water with her hand. "Mmm, nice," she murmured. She'd always wanted one of these things. This one was sparkling clean and smelled fresh. Tony must use it a lot, she mused. She wondered what kind of swimsuit he wore. Or maybe he didn't wear one at all....

Enough of that line of thinking! She needed something else to keep her mind and body occupied. Ah, the breakfast dishes. The tray was probably still up in Tony's room.

"Don't mind me," she said as she passed quietly through the living room.

He didn't. In fact, he seemed to have forgotten her existence entirely.

Well, what did she want, his undying gratitude? she berated herself as she went into the bedroom to retrieve the tray of dishes. She wasn't here for accolades. She was here to make his injury a little less inconvenient, to ease the burden she'd foisted upon him with her careless behavior last night. He didn't owe her thanks for doing what was fair and right.

His sheets were all rumpled, and Delia, robbed of her normal control by exhaustion, had no trouble remembering what the bed had looked like with Tony in it. Now that she was alone, she closed her eyes and savored the memory. It was a dangerous fantasy, but preferable to other, less pleasant thoughts she still didn't want to face.

Without really meaning to, she sank onto the edge of the modern platform bed, picked up the one remaining pillow that Tony hadn't taken downstairs and hugged it to her. It carried his scent, subtle and spicy and all male. She pressed her face against it and closed her eyes. All she wanted was to enfold herself in that scent as if it were Tony's arms.

Normally Delia was quite content to stand on her own two feet and take on whatever the world threw at her. But there were times, like now, when her doubts and fears threatened to close in around her and she needed someone to just hold her close. Knowing that another human being cared about her went a long way toward chasing off the things that scared her. Right now, she wanted that person to be Tony Griffin.

"Delia, you're a fool," she muttered to herself. Even if she and Tony had known each other on such a personal level, he wasn't the sympathetic type. He had shown no compassion for that poor woman whose brother had died. Why would he give a damn about Delia Pryde's trivial fears?

She wouldn't be thinking such crazy things about him if she weren't so tired. Yes, that was it. She was exhausted enough now that nothing would stand in the way of sleep. She would finish these dishes, maybe put in another load of wash, then get the hell out of here . . . as soon as she summoned the energy to stand up.

Tony whooped loudly enough to shake the roof when a rookie defensive end caught an interception and ran it in sixty yards for a Cowboys' touchdown. The score pushed the Dallas team ahead by four points, with less than two minutes left.

"Hey, Delia, you ought to come see this replay," he called out. "Even if you're not a football fan. It's a dream catch."

She didn't answer.

"Delia?" Come to think of it, he hadn't seen her lately. Oh, he'd been plenty aware of her whereabouts for a while, though he'd pretended disinterest. When she'd leaned over to set his cold drink on the table, he'd caught an intriguing glimpse of the shadowy valley between her breasts. And when she'd sashayed back toward the kitchen, his gaze had been glued to the gentle sway of her softly rounded derriere. Even the action on his TV screen hadn't been able to completely distract him from the sounds Delia had made as she worked in the laundry room. His eyes had been drawn to the flash of yellow he could see through the window out onto the patio, when she'd watered his plants. When she'd gone upstairs, her footsteps overhead had claimed part of his attention.

But that was the last he'd seen or heard of her, and that was almost an hour ago. "Delia!" he called again. No response.

She must have left, he concluded as the heaviness of disappointment settled in his chest. Well, that was exactly what he'd wanted, right? With his rude, demanding behavior he'd driven her away. Hopefully he'd also rid her of her guilt.

Tony watched the rest of the game with waning enthusiasm. His headache was back in full force and he was hungry again. He went into the kitchen and grabbed an apple from the fridge. As he crunched into it, he leaned his head around the corner to the laundry room. Hmm, she hadn't made much headway, and he couldn't blame her. That was some pretty disgusting laundry.

Feeling a bit guilty himself, he used his good arm to transfer into the dryer the clothes she had washed, then started another load. The cast wasn't as much of an inconvenience as he'd feared.

That done, he yawned and stretched expansively. Maybe he'd go back to bed and try to sleep off this headache. He retrieved the blanket and pillows from the couch and headed upstairs.

He saw her the moment he turned on the bedroom light. She was curled up in a tight ball on his bed, a pillow clutched to her chest. The bronze curtain of her hair spilled over one shoulder, the curled ends touching her cheek.

She looked so small and vulnerable that, once again, he felt the ancient male urge to protect her. But who would protect her from him? He'd never wanted any woman as desperately as he did this delicate butterfly.

But he couldn't have her now. She was exhausted, having evidently collapsed here without meaning to. She hadn't even taken off her shoes. Why hadn't he noticed the bluish shadows under her eyes before?

The pillows and blanket he held dropped to the floor unheeded. "Delia?"

She didn't stir.

Terrific. He'd been trying to get her to run screaming from his house, and instead she'd crawled into his bed. Twice he reached for her shoulder, intending to shake her awake, and twice he stopped himself. He couldn't bring himself to disturb her. Instead he moved the breakfast tray off the bed, then pulled off her tennis shoes. He draped the blanket over her and slipped a pillow under her head, allowing his hand to linger on one ivory cheek. Appropriately, her skin felt as soft as a butterfly's wing.

She made a few drowsy, fretful noises, enough to let him know that her sleep wasn't peaceful, but she didn't come close to consciousness.

Now what? After a brief battle with his conscience, Tony walked around the foot of the bed to the other side. He was just enough of a rogue that he could climb under the covers beside her without a qualm. Hell, as tired as she was, she'd never even know he was there. Still, he was just enough of a gentleman to keep his pants on.

Delia awoke suddenly with a numbing terror pressing in on her from all sides. The murder scene was fresh on her mind, as if she were still standing in the doorway of that blood-strewn apartment. She could even hear the sister's pitiful wailing, echoing in her ears.

"Delia! Delia, honey, it's all right. It was only a nightmare."

She understood then that the wailing came from her own throat. With an effort she quieted herself. Coming more fully awake, she also realized where she was and who was beside her in the bed.

"Delia, are you okay?" Tony rubbed gently, comforting circles between her shoulder blades with the heel of his hand.

"I . . . I think so," she managed between ragged breaths.

"Must have been one helluva dream." He reached to the nightstand and turned on a lamp. The warm glow chased away the shadows in the corners of the room as well as those in Delia's mind.

"It wasn't just a dream."

He nodded knowingly. "You were remembering last night?"

"Yes. God, it was so horrible, Tony. I never imagined, never guessed anything could look so awful. I mean, minutes before we got there he was a living, breathing human being. And then to see him reduced to *that* . . ." The weight in her chest grew heavier. She didn't want to cry, but every time she thought of that scene, her throat tightened.

"Shh, it's okay, honey," Tony said, drawing her against his chest.

She didn't resist. It was what she wanted, what she needed right now. "How do you do it?" she asked.

"Do what?"

"Face that sort of thing."

"Listen, I've been a cop for thirteen years. You get used to it. I know it wasn't a particularly pretty sight, but I've seen worse—multiple slayings, women, children, bodies that have been lying around for—"

"Tony! You've not helping."

"Sorry. But the point is, after a while that stuff doesn't affect you like it does at first. There's no room for emotion in police work, Delia. A cop has to be tough. That's the only way to get the job done."

After a long pause, she said quietly but distinctly, "No, you're wrong."

"What makes you think so?"

"My uncle who raised me. He's a cop. And one thing he's stressed to me over the years is the importance of the human element in police work. Caring about people is what motivates an officer to do his best work."

"Caring just gets in the way of a clear head," Tony argued. "How useful do you think I would be as a cop if I fell to pieces every time I saw a murder victim? I mean, let's face it, you were the one about to pass out, and you didn't do anyone any favors."

She stiffened at the reminder of her less-than-admirable part in last night's drama. "Maybe we're talking about two different things," she said, weighing her words carefully. "A person can't always control his physiological reactions. But as for compassion—I wanted to help that poor woman. I wanted to offer some comfort. And I might have been able to, if you'd let me." Delia's tone was faintly accusatory.

"Should I have dropped everything and let her cry on my shoulder? There was work to be done—urgent work."

"No, of course you shouldn't have dropped everything. But you might have told her you were sorry for her loss. And you might have touched her, squeezed her hand or her shoulder. It would have taken no more than a few seconds. Instead, you barked at her not to touch anything."

Had he behaved that coldly? he wondered. "It was important to secure the scene," he rationalized. "There was valuable evidence—"

"That woman had just witnessed her brother's brutal murder," Delia interrupted. "Do you think she gave a damn about *evidence?* All the evidence in the world couldn't bring him back. She needed to know that someone cared, and she didn't have anyone to help her through it. She didn't have anyone, Tony."

Delia couldn't stem the flow of tears, so she let them fall this time.

Tony responded by tightening his hold on her and stroking her hair with his other hand. His clumsy efforts were made even clumsier by the cast on his arm. He simply wasn't good at this sort of thing, but still he tried. Delia had awakened the strangest instincts in him, long dormant but definitely alive.

"You're right, you know," he murmured when her racking sobs had subsided, replaced by occasional, muffled sniffs.

"I . . . I am?"

"Partly, anyway. It's not the first time I've been called hard-hearted. But I've also been called a pretty good cop. I have to do what works for me." He didn't add that once upon a time, when he was a rookie, he'd been called just the opposite—too softhearted and a lousy cop.

The chief himself had spent the better part of an hour raking Tony over the coals for staying with a frightened, elderly couple while an armed robber got away clean. "You have all the crime-fighting instincts of a mother hen," Chief Quimby had seethed. It was then that Tony had seen the light. Yes, he had offered those old people a little short-term comfort, but he would have served them far better by catching the robber and getting back their money and jewelry.

Gradually he had learned to adjust his priorities and toughen his heart. It hadn't made him a popular guy, but he had a hell of a good arrest record.

But how could someone like Delia, whose emotions were constantly right at the surface, understand his philosophy?

"Every time I let myself care too much, it gets me in trouble," he ventured.

"Are you trying to convince me, or yourself?"

"I don't have to convince myself. All I have to do is remember last night. I worried about you, about your feelings, rather than doing my job, and I got careless. And you saw what happened then."

"You should have let me alone. I'd have managed."

He sighed. "I couldn't." And that was the hell of it. The moment he'd started to care about Delia, even a tiny bit, he'd opened Pandora's box. Now he couldn't seem to stop.

"Does it ever get better?" she asked.

"I sure hope so."

"I mean, the memory is so vivid. Does it ever fade?"

"Oh. Of course it does," he said. "Give it some time. You'll be fine."

"In the beginning, before you got used to the violence, how did you deal with it?"

He had to think back. But then he remembered a little trick he used to play with his own mind. He hadn't thought about it in years. "I used to tell myself that it didn't make any difference whether I witnessed an ugly scene or not. The scene would still be there, the people still dead, the blood still as red, regardless of whether I was there to see it. Sounds silly, but it helped me." He used to chant it like a mantra.

"It doesn't sound silly. I'll try it." She picked at a loose thread on the blanket and cleared her throat a couple of times. "Umm, Tony, what are you doing in bed with me?"

He'd been wondering when she'd get around to that question. "I might ask you the same thing," he said. "It is *my* bed, after all."

"I was here first," she pointed out.

"Yes, you were," he said thoughtfully. "Pity you fell asleep before I arrived." He continued to absently fondle her silky hair as his words hung heavy between them.

Her objection, when it came, was strident. "Of all the—" She pulled away from him. "I had no intention of... It figures you would think the worst of me. But I was so tired..." Her words trailed off when he started to laugh.

She socked him in the ribs, just hard enough to make him stop. "Quit trying to embarrass me."

"I only wanted to get your mind off the murder. Nothing takes away the heebie-jeebies like a good head of steam. You do feel better now, don't you?"

She went all soft again, her brief spurt of outrage spent. "Yes, but more because you let me cry all over you than anything." She touched his still-damp chest with her fingertips.

Something pulled tight as piano wire deep inside Tony's body. Cripes, the woman had no idea what she was doing to him. He took her hand in his and gently drew it away. "You needed to cry," he said. "Just like you needed to sleep. Oh, and for the record, I didn't flatter myself that you'd crawled into my bed with seduction in mind, not when you were still fully dressed right down to your shoes."

She wiggled her feet beneath the blanket. "You took them off, didn't you? And you gave me an extra pillow and covered me up. I'm supposed to be taking care of you."

"I tried to wake you," he said gruffly. "You were dead to the world. And don't be painting me as some sort of saint. After all, I did get into bed with you, and without your consent."

"Yes, you did. Should I worry?"

He smiled. "Possibly. I don't intend to spend the rest of the night in these jeans."

His subtle threat didn't budge her an inch. "We've never even kissed." With those few quiet words, she moved them from the realm of idle teasing to one of possibilities.

Tony's blood quickened. "I can remedy that." He curled his good arm around her neck and tipped her head back. He searched her blue eyes for some sign of hesitancy, and found only willingness. She offered her mouth to his as sweetly as she might have offered a flower or a song. And though it cost him, he was careful not to abuse her gift. The touch of his lips to hers was gentle, an inquisitive testing of the softness there. She tasted sweet and smelled of innocence.

It was Delia who deepened the kiss, weaving her fingers through his hair and pulling him closer, teasing him with quick darting movements of her tongue. He could feel the warm globes of her breasts pressed against him, and more than anything he wanted to touch them. He brushed the side of one with his fingertips and silently cursed the cast on his arm. Delia's beautiful breasts were there for the taking, and the best he could do was scratch at them like a dog.

Reading his mind, she broke the kiss and pulled away from him, easing his good arm from around her shoulders. Wordlessly she brought his hand to her breast and held it there, all the while looking into his eyes as if for approval.

"Oh, yes, Delia," he said, inexplicably moved by the simple gesture. Even through the yellow knit of her sweat suit, her flesh felt warm and alive against his palm.

"It feels good, you touching me."

"Then I'll keep doing it. I'll touch you anyplace you want."

"And will you make love to me?" she asked, almost desperately.

"I'd like nothing better," he said, tamping down the white-hot excitement that threatened to explode inside him at the mere thought. He had to force out his next few words. "Delia, are you sure? I want you more than anything, but you've known me barely twenty-four hours."

"I know all I need to know about you, and I've never been more sure of anything. And if you're worried about taking advantage of an unhinged woman,.

don't. I'm calm now, I'm rational, and I've wanted you since five minutes after we met. Now it's beyond that. I need you tonight, Tony. Way down deep, I need you to hold me, 'cause when you hold me and kiss me I can't think of anything but you and how wonderful you make me feel. There's no room for anything else. I won't have any regrets, I promise.''

Now he understood—only too well. She needed him to keep the demons at bay. He'd never experienced the syndrome himself but he'd heard of it. When someone brushed death too closely, they needed to reaffirm life as quickly and intensely as possible. And what better way to do that than to make love?

Tony frowned. It wasn't him Delia needed, per se. She simply needed to be loved and loved well. So he didn't bother with the usual cautions he might have offered. He didn't remind her that he had nothing to give in the way of a lasting relationship. He didn't warn her that he wasn't in the market for a wife or even a serious lover. He simply took her in his arms and kissed her very soundly, very thoroughly.

Five

Tony's kiss was hot and deep and demanding, not at all like his first, tender exploration. Delia lost herself in it, falling headfirst into an abyss of exquisite sensations. Led by instinct, she met his questing tongue with her own in a sensual dance, challenging, retreating, engaging in a battle neither of them would lose.

There was no hesitancy, no doubt on Delia's part. Though their physical relationship was exploding with unprecedented suddenness, she felt a sense of rightness about it.

She wasn't foolish enough to believe Tony harbored any deep feelings toward her. They hadn't known each other long enough for that. What she did sense was a certain compassion, a capacity for tenderness that he kept well guarded. She intended to uncover that tenderness and experience it to its fullest.

She hoped that perhaps this night would lead to more just like it, that she and Tony would have the chance to explore the potential between them. But if it didn't—if this shadowy encounter was to be their only one—she would never regret it. Already she knew that. She needed him. She needed him to heal her bruised psyche.

Her restless hands searched out the subtle textures of his hair and the corded muscles of his neck. He groaned with pleasure when she touched his ear, so she made a point of investigating its contours, first with her fingertips, then with her tongue. She smiled in secret delight when he grew very still, as if he were devoting his total consciousness to the sensations her simple efforts brought to him.

But he didn't remain still for long. Before Delia knew what was happening, he shifted his weight, pressing her back against the pillows. Then she was once again the one drowning in pleasure as he indulged her with slow, warm kisses. Even handicapped as he was, with only one good hand, he managed to caress her in the most creative and satisfying ways. He grazed his fingertips along her jaw, down her neck, in the hollow of her throat. His touch dipped below the neckline of her top to tease the valley between her breasts, then toyed with the zipper tab.

"Are you going to take this off for me?" he asked.

The huskiness in his voice affected her in ways she hadn't imagined. The heat at the core of her femininity intensified until it formed a glowing ball of fire deep inside of her.

"Well, yes, I was planning to take off my clothes at some point. But . . . the light . . ."

"I want to see you. You aren't going all shy on me, are you?" He smoothed a strand of her hair behind her ear.

"Not shy," she denied quickly, even though she was suddenly, desperately afraid to reveal her body to him. Where she'd had no doubts before, now her mind whirled with them. She wanted to please him, to make their coming together as glorious for him as she knew it would be for her. "It's just that the light's shining in my eyes," she finished lamely.

"Then don't look at it. Look at me instead." He teased her with a smile as he inched the zipper down, just enough to reveal her lacy bra, then paused. "You do the rest. I'm too clumsy with just one hand."

She sat up. Apparently he had a few doubts of his own, which only endeared him to her. "Trust me, you're not in the least clumsy," she said, lightly caressing his face. Then, with shaking hands, she finished the zipper and quickly shrugged the garment off her shoulders. Feeling brave, she unfastened the front clasp of her bra.

Tony took over from there, sliding his hand beneath the wisp of lace to cup her breast. "You're so beautiful," he said with unmistakable awe as he gently massaged her. "I've never seen skin like yours."

She eased the bra off her shoulders and tossed it aside, right along with her doubts. She'd been called pretty before, even beautiful. But never had she been so sure that a man meant what he said. She glowed with the pleasure of his approval.

He eased her down against the pillows once again, then bent over her and took her taut nipple in his mouth, and Delia thought she would dissolve in the heat he ignited. He explored her breasts with his hand, his mouth, his tongue, until she was sure he must have been trying to memorize the feel of them, the texture, the scent. So much attention he paid them, in fact, that she came near to swooning in anticipation of his devoting himself with the same generosity to the rest of her body.

Impatient now to have it all, she reached for the top button of his jeans. "I want to touch you. I want you to feel like you never have before. I want to give as good as I'm getting."

He stilled her almost frantic efforts. "Honey, you don't have to do a thing but lie there and you'll be giving me everything I could possibly want. Just let me, ah—oh!"

She had thrust her hand inside his jeans to boldly touch the hard length of him, and his surprised reaction pleased her enormously. "What was that you were saying?"

"You won't be so smug when you end things before they've even started, which is exactly what will happen if you keep that up." He grasped her wrist and gently but firmly pulled her hand away from him.

"So what?" she objected. "We've got all night. We'll start again."

"We've got all night," he agreed. "So don't rush me." With that, he rolled away from her and stood by the side of the bed. For a moment she was afraid she'd offended him somehow, but he erased her fears with that dazzling smile of his, and she realized he was standing so he could remove his snug jeans—a task he accomplished with some difficulty with only one good arm.

"Do you need help?" she asked, watching with frank admiration as he pulled the worn denim down his powerful thighs.

"Please, leave me some shred of manly pride," he said as he kicked the jeans aside. "I can at least take off my clothes by myself."

"But why would you want to, when you have someone so willing to provide assistance?" With that she rose to her knees and scooted to the side of the bed. She noted the momentary glint of apprehension in his dark eyes, and paused. "You're not used to a woman taking control, even for a few moments, are you?"

"It...it doesn't usually happen," he confessed. "That doesn't mean I don't like it." He grinned down at her and tousled her hair. "You're a surprise to me, Delia. All last night, I kept thinking how innocent you were."

"I am innocent," she said as she laid her palm against the rippling muscles of his abdomen. "Well, I'm not particularly experienced, anyway, and I've certainly never been very assertive when it came to...this sort of thing." She slipped her two forefingers under the waistband of his snowy briefs, one at each of his hipbones. "This just feels right to me. I can't explain why." Slowly she lowered the soft cotton, freeing his magnificent arousal.

He was beautiful—there was no other word for it. The firmness of his body, the finely sculpted planes of muscle and especially the latent power she sensed filled her with a whirlwind of heat and longing.

"Now you, honey," he said.

He didn't have to ask twice. With an economy of movement she whisked off her sweatpants, underwear and socks in one graceful sweep and flung them aside. Tony's fathomless eyes followed her every movement, revealing a growing hunger. She basked in the heat of it.

"Come stand beside me for a minute," he said.

She obeyed without question.

"Put your arms around my neck."

She did. And then he pulled her body flush against his and kissed her with enough passion to make her head reel. She was acutely aware of every inch of her skin that touched his—the rough hair of his chest against her breasts, the hot throb of his arousal against her abdomen, his strong hand on her hip. The fiberglass cast bit into her where he had wrapped his arm around her shoulders, but she hardly noticed the slight discomfort.

He broke the kiss, breathing heavily. "I want you, Delia. I can't wait any longer."

"You don't have to wait." She sank onto the bed because her knees wouldn't hold her up any longer. Leaning back, she held out her hand in a silent invitation to lie with her. With a low growl of approval he covered her with the warmth and security of his body, gently nudging her legs apart so that he could nestle in the cradle she made there.

She was amazed at how smoothly they fit together. There was no fumbling, no hesitation, no adjustments to be made. He just slid into her, filling her with his need, and she wrapped her legs around his hips and rocked with him.

His gaze never left hers as he surged deeply inside her. He didn't kiss her, but he didn't have to. An intensity shined from his eyes, emotions so profound, they brought Delia to tears. This was what she needed—proof that even a tough guy like Tony Griffin could be tender, gentle and loving in his own way.

She wasn't thinking about sexual fulfillment. In the past she'd always had to try for it, to concentrate her mind fully on her own pleasure in order to achieve it. Tonight, all she wanted was to fill her mind with Tony and the strange, wonderful feelings he brought to her body and spirit. So when the physical climax came, it took her totally unaware. She cried out with the violence of the explosion, and as she savored the waves of ecstasy coursing through her in ever-widening circles, she was vaguely aware that Tony had reached his own summit.

There were no words between them for the longest time, but none were necessary. Delia was fairly sure that something far out of the ordinary had transpired between them, and she was almost afraid to break the magic spell by speaking of it. Mere words just wouldn't do justice to the experience. So, except for a sigh of supreme contentment, she remained silent.

It was Tony who finally spoke. "You still with me?"

"Mmm-hmm." *As long as you'll have me,* some inner voice added.

"Do you feel better?" He planted a light kiss on her forehead.

"Better than I ever have in my life."

He couldn't help but smile with male satisfaction. "Good. I know my headache's gone."

Delia was immediately contrite. "Oh, your poor head. I forgot all about it." She brushed his damp hair away from the ugly purple bruise on his forehead.

"There's nothing 'poor' about my head or any other part of me, thanks to you. You cold?"

"Mmm, a little."

Tony drew the covers up and tucked them around Delia's shoulders, snuggling her close to his chest. She sighed again and was soon breathing the slow, deep breaths of untroubled sleep. She didn't stir when he reached over to turn off the lamp.

It took Tony a while longer to escape his own restless thoughts into the oblivion of sleep. He was acutely aware of the small, still form that fit so neatly against him—not so much in a sexual way just now, but in a protective way. She seemed fragile, even when she showed the strength of character that was so much a part of her.

He felt that Delia had given him a precious gift—her beautiful body, of course, but more importantly, her trust. That affected him in ways he'd never dreamed. He had expected to enjoy making love to her, but he'd never imagined that she would open him up inside the way she had. He felt as if a dam somewhere inside him were crumbling away, and the rush of what was behind that dam scared him a little.

Delia woke up unusually happy, and it took her a moment to realize why. Then she saw Tony lying on his stomach next to her, his head burrowed under his pillow, and she remembered.

She grinned unabashedly as scenes from last night whirled through her mind, a kaleidoscope of wondrous sensations. The other memories were there, too—the bad ones—but they had faded in intensity. They were losing their ugly grip on her.

She would have stayed where she was, but she didn't want to wake Tony and she had no idea how long he would sleep. Besides, the lure of a warm shower beckoned.

She slipped out of bed and opened Tony's closet, hoping he wouldn't mind her presumption, and after a moment found just what she wanted, a paisley silk robe. Judging from its location at the very back of the closet, he didn't wear it much. A little too fussy for him, she decided. She draped the cool silk over her arm and headed for the bathroom.

Tony had been seesawing back and forth between waking and sleeping ever since dawn. Each time he awakened, he would reach out and lightly touch Delia's warm body. Reassured that she wasn't just a pleasant dream, he would drift back to sleep. This time when he reached out, however, he found the space beside him empty. He wrenched his eyes open and searched for Delia in a momentary panic. Then he heard the water running and he relaxed.

Still nude, he padded to the bathroom door and opened it a crack. "Delia?"

"Good morning," she trilled back.

"You always wake up cheerful?"

"Uh-huh. Do you? If not, maybe I could cheer you up. That plastic thing to cover up your cast is sitting right by the sink."

So it was.

"I'll scrub your back," she said with a teasing lilt.

She'd hardly gotten the invitation out before he was standing there with her under the warm spray, greeting her with his best good-morning kiss. "This is an ungodly hour for me to be up," he told her.

She just smiled serenely and instructed him to turn around. Then she proceeded to scrub his back and several other places, as well, working the slick soap over his skin with clever, purposeful hands.

"Mmm, my turn," he said, grinning mischievously as he swiveled to face her. Just then the shower spray turned abruptly cold. Delia squeaked in surprise and Tony made a dive for the faucet knobs.

"Small water heater," he apologized. "It's on my list of improvements to be made."

"'S okay," she said, shivering as she stepped out of the shower and found a towel.

Tony dried himself quickly, then hung his damp towel over the shower rod. When Delia started to wrap hers around herself, he gently took it from her and tossed it aside. "You don't need that if we're going back to bed, do you?"

She gave her head a saucy toss, her wet hair sending water droplets in every direction. "I guess what they say about cold showers isn't always true."

"Not in this case." After allowing her hands to roam over him, nothing would cool him down except to find release with her.

As Delia stood in front of Tony's washing machine, wearing his silk robe, it occurred to her that she hadn't eaten anything the day before. She was famished! She quickly put in another load of laundry, including her own things, then returned to the kitchen where Tony was struggling to make coffee.

"Need some help?" she asked. "Or am I trampling on your manly pride again?"

"I'll get it," he grumbled, doggedly spooning grounds into a paper filter with his left hand. "Then again, maybe we should go out to breakfast."

"Not unless you want me to go like this," she said, opening the refrigerator. "I just put my clothes in the washer. I'll make something here, if that's okay." He offered no objections, so she scavenged the last two bagels, sliced them and popped them into the toaster. "Soon as my clothes are done, I'll be out of your hair." She tossed the words out with more casualness than she felt, knowing that as soon as she left, the spell would be broken.

"I like you in my hair. For that matter, I like being in your hair." He came up behind her and laced his fingers through her still-damp curls, then lifted the heavy amber mass off her neck and kissed her nape.

She shivered with renewed desire. Lord, they'd just gotten out of bed. How could she want him again so quickly?

"It's Monday," he said when she didn't respond. "I guess you have things to do."

"Mmm-hmm. But if you need me to help out with anything—"

"No, Delia, you've done more than enough. I shouldn't have asked you to do all that work—the laundry, the plants—"

"I fell asleep before I could do much," she pointed out.

"I'm glad you did."

The simple statement gave her slight comfort. What she really wanted was to know whether he ever wanted to see her again. But that was probably a futile wish. Tony was a little too tough on the outside to admit to any sort of emotional attachment, or even a weakness of the flesh. She could almost hear him telling her that their coming together was simply a case of mutual need, mutual satisfaction of desires. Personally, she believed it was more. Or that it could become more. But she was too chicken to bring up the subject.

When they were seated across from each other crunching on bagels with cream cheese and jam, she asked, "You've never been married, have you? Oh, don't worry, I'm not trying to corral you into making an honest woman of me," she quipped. "I'm just rudely curious, that's all."

The question didn't seem to bother him much. "Nope, never been married. Probably never will be. Marriages and police work are a risky combination, especially the shifts I cover. I never figured it'd work out."

"Have you ever come close?" she asked.

That query made him squirm a bit. "Once, a long time ago. She wanted me to give up the Southeast Division, though. Said she wouldn't be able to sleep at night knowing I was out on the streets of South Dallas. Guess I couldn't blame her. But I couldn't see myself patrolling some ritzy neighborhood up north where nothing ever happens. So we didn't get married."

"Mmm, I guess some cops get addicted to the action."

"It's not just that. I feel a real loyalty to the people on my beat. I like doing my small part to clean up the streets for them. Of course, it's an uphill battle. For every drug dealer we put in jail, another takes his place." He sighed.

So, police work was more than just a job for Tony, Delia mused. He believed in trying to right the wrongs of the world, no matter how difficult the challenge, just as her Uncle Tab did. Just as she did. The small insight made her feel closer to him.

The dryer buzzed. Without a word, Delia rose and went to take care of the laundry. Another few min-

utes and her things would be dry, and then she would
have to go home. She dreaded that moment not only
because she didn't want to leave Tony, but because
when she got home there would undoubtedly be a
message on her answering machine from Uncle Tab.
She would have to face his disapproval sooner or later,
but she wished it could be later.

She was on her way upstairs to make the bed and
straighten the bathroom when the doorbell rang. Curious, she turned to the front door and peered through
the peephole. Her stomach sank all the way to her an-
kles.

Tony appeared in the entry hall. As soon as he saw
her, his brow creased with concern. "What's wrong,
Delia? Who is it?"

"It's my uncle," she groaned. "What terrible timing!"

"Your uncle?" Tony looked out the peephole himself. "That's not your uncle, it's the chief...." His eyes
widened in horror as realization dawned. "Shenniker's your uncle?"

Delia bit her lower lip. "'Fraid so."

The betrayal she saw in Tony's eyes cut through her
like the sharp edge of a diamond.

"I was going to tell you, Tony—"

"Save it for my eulogy," he barked as he opened the
door. In a slightly more civilized tone he said,
"'Morning, Chief."

"Well, glad to see you're up and around." Tab
Shenniker was a big man with a big voice, which
boomed through the entryway. "Mind if I come in?"

Delia toyed with the idea of fleeing upstairs before
her uncle saw her. Her immediate disappearance
would save a lot of embarrassment. But it occurred to

her that Tony might need her to help explain what had happened Saturday night. The last thing she wanted was for him to be blamed for something that was essentially her fault. So she stood her ground.

Tony opened the door wider, throwing Delia one final, censorious glare before her uncle stepped inside and caught sight of her.

"Dee?" His bushy white eyebrows flew upward. "What in the name of heaven are you doing here? And dressed like *that?*"

"I spent the night here," she said, knowing nothing but the truth would work. "I was helping Tony out. With that arm laid up, he needed someone to cook and do a few chores. And he was helping me out. After the things I saw, I didn't want to be alone." That was pretty much the truth, and it was as specific as she was going to get.

"If you were upset, you could have come to see me," her uncle groused. "It's not like I haven't seen terrible things. I could have helped you through it."

"After you'd given me a good long lecture, perhaps," she conceded dryly.

"You don't need to cut me up with your sharp tongue on top of everything else." He gave her a look that spoke of dire consequences, but that was the last he had to say about her sleeping arrangements, for now. His relatively mild reaction surprised her. She had expected him to raise the roof. He still might, she mused unhappily. He'd hardly gotten warmed up yet.

Tab shifted his attention to Tony. "What do I have to do to get a cup of coffee around here?"

Tony looked as uncomfortable as a man could get. "This way." He led the way through the living room and into the kitchen.

Delia automatically assumed the role of hostess, pouring coffee for the two men and then refilling her own mug. Even if it wasn't exactly proper etiquette, the activity helped to steady her nerves.

"Well, I read the initial report on Saturday night's incident," Tab began when they'd all settled around the small kitchen table. "Highly sanitized, I suspect. Now, Sergeant Griffin, do you want to tell me what really happened? Let's start with something simple, like…what in the hell were you thinking, to allow my niece in your patrol car on a Saturday night in South Dallas?"

"Begging your pardon, sir, but I didn't know she was your niece."

"He didn't," Delia chimed in.

"I've got pictures of her all over my office," Tab objected, virtually ignoring his niece. "How could you not recognize her, man?"

"The most recent picture you have of me is from high school," Delia pointed out. "With that, and our last names being different, and you always calling me Dee instead of Delia, it's no wonder Tony didn't make the connection."

Tab placed the flats of his hands on the tabletop, as if to prevent himself from letting them stray to Delia's neck. "I would appreciate it, Dee, if you would let Sergeant Griffin speak for himself."

"I'm just trying to clarify things."

"When I want your clarification, I'll ask for it," Tab said with a menacing stare. Oh, he was angry, all right. Delia couldn't remember ever seeing him quite so incensed. So she took a sip of her coffee and kept quiet, for the time being.

"So even if you didn't know who she was," he continued, his cutting blue eyes focused on Tony, "couldn't you see she was just a young girl? She had no business riding with you. None at all!"

"If it had been up to me, I'd have sent her home," Tony said quietly.

Young girl? Sent her home? Delia tucked the injustices away to deal with later. She didn't figure either man would care to be reminded just now that she was an adult, and had been for some time.

"Are you telling me you had no choice in the matter?"

"That's right."

"By whose order?"

Tony hesitated, obviously not wanting to get his immediate superior into hot water.

"Oh, never mind," Tab said, shaking his head in disgust. "So you were ordered to take her along, and you're a man who follows orders. I'll give you that. Still, did you have to take her to a bloody shooting?"

"I was the closest unit to the crime," Tony explained. "I told Delia to stay in the car, but..."

"I didn't listen," Delia blurted out, no longer able to keep silent. "Uncle Tab, it was all my fault. Tony didn't want me on patrol with him—that was plain from the beginning. But I insisted, and then I wouldn't stay in the car when he told me to. I wanted to see what was going on. I wanted to prove to you and to myself that I was tough. But I didn't know it would be so bad...and then I started to feel sick and Tony was worried about me, and the next thing I knew this man came rushing out of the shadows and... Please, Uncle Tab, it wasn't Tony's fault. I was in the way, and I distracted him from his duty, and . . . and . . ." To her horror, tears sprang into her eyes.

Tony's reaction to her outburst surprised her. He took her hand. "Delia, look at me," he commanded.

She did, and suddenly it was as if they were the only two people there.

"I want you to stop blaming yourself for what happened. Perhaps you did make a small error in judgment. And I have to accept some of the blame—I *allowed* myself to be distracted. But mostly it was just plain old rotten luck. That guy with the gun might have surprised me regardless of whether you were there. If not me, then some other officer. Do you understand that?"

"That's not what you said before." She swiped at her tears before they could escape down her cheeks.

"I was angry and frustrated before, and I had a headache. I also found it easier to blame you than myself. I'm sorry, okay?"

She nodded, unable to speak. She hadn't realized how badly she needed to hear those words, to know that Tony didn't hold her totally responsible for his injuries.

"Good." He gave her hand a brief squeeze before releasing it.

Delia was vaguely aware of her uncle watching them carefully. She opened her mouth, intending to again plead with him not to punish Tony for an incident he couldn't have prevented, when the clothes dryer buzzed. Taking it as a reprieve from the heavens, she quickly excused herself. She would stand a better chance of stating her case if she composed herself first.

Tony watched her go, the soft silk of her robe whispering around her shapely legs as she walked, and he

admired her as he never had before. Tab Shenniker's
temper wasn't something you invited, and yet Delia
had sat here and calmly tried to accept the entire blame
for Saturday night. He didn't know whether she really felt that way or whether she was just being noble
by attempting to save his hide. Either way, at that
moment he adored her.

"You have a strange look in your eye when you
watch her," Shenniker commented.

"I'm not surprised," Tony responded. "She's a
strange woman—um, no disrespect intended."

"None taken," Shenniker said affably. He got up
and poured himself another cup of coffee. "You forget, I've known her since she was seven. Even then she
had a will of her own, insisting she wouldn't come
home with me unless her cat came with us. An ugly,
mangy thing it was, too, and I hate cats."

"But it came with you."

"Exactly. When she wants something bad enough,
she usually gets it. That's what scares me so much
about her wanting to go into police work. Her inten-
tions are noble, of course, but anybody can see that
she's not equipped to handle such a rough job."

Tony nodded his agreement.

"And yet, when she told me how much respect she
had for me and my career, and how she wanted to play
a meaningful role in fighting crime, she had that gleam
in her eye, the one that tells me she won't let anything
stand in her way."

Tony was quite familiar with that gleam himself.
"Frankly, I don't think you have anything to worry
about," he said. "Not after Saturday night."

"I understand the murder scene was a bad one."

"Worse than most. It even gave me a turn," Tony admitted.

"Then perhaps everything's worked out for the best," Shenniker said thoughtfully, "if this fiasco has convinced her that joining the police force is a damn fool notion."

"I'm sure it has." He gave a short laugh. "Can you imagine, Delia turned loose on the streets with a gun and a badge?" Before the words were even out of his mouth, Tony was uncomfortably aware that he'd been overheard. Delia stood in the doorway between the kitchen and utility room, dressed once again in her buttery yellow warm-ups, and she was fuming.

"You're both wrong," she said in a tight voice as she bent down to tie her tennis shoes. "You can laugh if you want, but I have every intention of pursuing a law-enforcement career. I passed all the entrance tests. I came through my interview with the board just fine. My training begins after Christmas."

Tony sprang out of his chair, unsure what he wanted to do. "You can't be serious!"

"I most certainly am," she said in a voice laced with steel. "Maybe I don't know how to handle myself in every situation, but I'll go to the police academy and I'll learn, just like the both of you did. I'm sorry if you don't approve, Uncle Tab, but there's nothing you can do to stop me. Nothing either of you can do."

On that note she whisked herself out of the room. Seconds later the front door slammed. Tony wondered bleakly if Delia had just whisked herself out of his life, as well.

Six

———

At the end of the half-mile run, all Delia wanted to do was drop to the ground in exhaustion. It was thirty-five degrees outside—cold for Dallas, even in January—and Delia was wringing with perspiration while her heart raced alarmingly.

She had been jogging on her own for weeks and hadn't expected to have any trouble with this part of her training. But the group's pace was faster than what she was used to.

Looking around her, she noted that none of the other fifty-two recruits in her class appeared to be unduly winded. Delia, on the other hand, was puffing like an old steam locomotive. She tried to gasp quietly as she followed the group into the training center so as not to draw attention to her distress.

Sylvia Mendez, one of the other eight woman recruits in the class, punched Delia playfully on the shoulder. "What a way to start the day, huh? I love running. My favorite part of military training were those five- and ten-mile runs."

Delia nodded numbly. Sylvia was a big, jovial woman, a former marine, and she was as gung ho about training as a cadet could get. She already knew how to shoot a gun, and from the looks of her she could probably wrestle a grizzly bear to the ground and handcuff it. Delia knew she could learn a lot from Sylvia. But frankly, the woman intimidated her. Walking beside Sylvia, she felt like someone's little sister tagging along with the big kids.

Delia's next hurdle was a half hour of grueling calisthenics. At the end of forty sit-ups and twenty push-ups she did collapse, for a few moments at least. Her arms felt like mush and she knew her face must be tomato red.

"Hey, Pryde, we only got five minutes before the defense training starts," Sylvia boomed from above Delia's prostrate form. "Don't you want to get a drink of water or something? You look like you could use one."

"I'm okay," Delia said as she accepted Sylvia's helping hand up. But she wasn't really. She was tired, shaky and a little scared. This was her first day of physical training, the first *hour* of her first day, and she was half-dead. How was she supposed to survive twenty-eight more weeks of this stuff?

"You're not in such hot shape." Sylvia observed as they stood in line at the drinking fountain.

"I thought I was," Delia admitted, trying not to take offense. Her new friend had only stated the obvious. "I've been running a little, you know, and doing some aerobics with a video, but I guess it wasn't enough." She stepped up to the drinking fountain and gulped down some tepid water. "It gets better, right?"

Sylvia clicked her tongue and shook her head. "It gets worse before it gets better. But you can make it if you're really determined. Listen, if you want, I can show you some things in the workout room after we're done today, some exercises that will make you stronger."

"Thanks, but when we get done today I'm going straight home and into a hot bath. I may stay there 'til tomorrow morning." She turned away from the fountain—and ran smack into a rock-hard pair of male pectorals. She took a step back and started to issue an automatic apology, but the words died in her throat when she recognized the face attached to the chest.

She hadn't seen or talked to Tony Griffin in two months, since the morning she'd made her pretty speech and stormed out of his house, but hardly an hour had gone by that he hadn't plagued her thoughts.

"Tony?" she managed to squeak.

"Hi, Delia." He smiled, more bemused than friendly.

She realized then what a mess she looked, with her hair pulled back into an untidy bun and perspiration dripping down her face. On top of that, she knew the police-issue blue shorts and shapeless gray T-shirt didn't do a thing for her.

Tony's similar attire, however, only accentuated his good points, revealing firm, athletic legs and delineating every gorgeous muscle in his upper torso. Delia found herself staring where she shouldn't, remembering the feel of those muscles beneath her hands. Quickly she focused her gaze on his right arm, noticeably thinner and paler than the other.

"I see you got your cast off," she said. "Is your wrist healing all right? I . . . I've been wondering."

"You could have picked up the phone and called to find out." He folded his arms and stared down at her with a definite hint of arrogance.

She gritted her teeth, refusing to let him bait her. "I thought about calling, but I didn't know how you'd take that. We didn't part on the best of terms." *And you could have called me,* she added silently.

"You were the one spouting off like a volcano," he pointed out.

"You were the one trying to tell me I wasn't cut out for police work!" All the anger and outrage she'd thought were dead and buried came boiling to the surface. "You and Uncle Tab talked about me like I was some disobedient—"

"Ah, yes, *Uncle* Tab. When were you planning to let me in on that little secret?"

She sighed with exasperation. Just when she was feeling her energy surge with self-righteousness, he had somehow managed to shift things so that she was the guilty party. "I was going to tell you," she said, glancing away and then back again. "It just wasn't very high on my priority list. Would it have made a difference?"

His dark eyes flashed with an instant of remembered passion so that Delia knew he understood exactly what she was asking: Would he still have made love to her?

"Aren't you going to introduce me to your friend?"

Delia and Tony shifted their gazes to Sylvia, who had a decidedly knowing look on her face.

Delia was grateful for the interruption. "Sylvia, this is Sergeant Tony Griffin. You might say he was instrumental in my decision to train for police work. Tony, Sylvia Mendez.''

Sylvia's handshake actually made Tony wince. "Good to meet you," she said. Then she turned to Delia. "We better get back. It's almost time."

Delia nodded, but her eye remained on Tony. "How is the arm?" she asked again. She was genuinely concerned, even if the big jerk didn't deserve such consideration. "You never did tell me."

"Not a hundred percent. That's why I'm here."

"Oh? What, you're using the weight room?"

"No, we have workout equipment at the station. I'm here as your defense-tactics instructor."

Delia's mouth opened, but no words came out.

"I can't return to patrol until I have all my strength back in my right hand. Since I hate desk work, your uncle suggested a teaching stint. I'm filling in for the regular instructor, who's recovering from surgery, so it works out well."

Now Delia saw things clearly. Lately, she and her uncle hadn't enjoyed a very warm relationship. In fact, they were barely speaking to one another. He was furious with her for going against his wishes, and now he was exacting revenge by siccing Tony on her—his personal watchdog.

The realization made her so irate, she couldn't even verbalize it. Better not to, anyway, she decided—not here. "I have to go," she said abruptly as she turned to join Sylvia, who was waiting and watching with curious eyes.

"That's one fine-looking hombre," Sylvia said when they were out of Tony's earshot.

"A fine-looking snake in the grass is what he is," Delia muttered. She had no opportunity to elaborate.

Tony had joined her basic training sergeant at the front of the room, and the class reconvened.

Of all the rotten luck, Delia ranted silently as she tried not to listen to the sergeant's glowing introduction of Tony. She was worried enough about the physical demands of training without this added anxiety. For eight weeks she'd been struggling to keep Tony Griffin off her mind. How could she possibly do that when he would be right there in front of her every day, flashing his muscles?

In her weaker moments, she had fantasized about how and when she and Tony would meet again. She'd seen herself as a successful graduate of the police academy, with a badge on her shirt and a gun in her holster, strolling into the Southeast Station and reporting to him for her field training. She'd never in her worst nightmares imagined they would meet again when she was tired, sweaty and discouraged.

There was no getting around it—for the next few weeks, Tony would see her every day at her *worst.*

It was better that way, she told herself. He wouldn't be tempted to recapture those brief moments of ecstasy they'd shared, and neither would she. She didn't need the distraction. All of her energy would have to go toward successfully completing her training.

When Tony took over the class, he explained that on this first day he would show them a sampling of the kinds of defense tactics he would teach them over the next few weeks. Then he assigned each recruit a partner to spar with.

"Pryde, you're with Mendez." His dark gaze lingered on her, and she felt as if she'd been physically caressed.

"Come on, partner," Sylvia said as she once again offered a hand-up to Delia.

"Not a very even match," Delia commented, shaking off what had to be a delusion brought on by exhaustion. Tony hadn't *really* singled her out for a smoldering stare. "You'll beat me to smithereens."

Sylvia smiled, obviously considering Delia's comment a compliment. "I'll go easy on you, at first. But you'll get tough. I predict that when training is over in the summer, you'll be able to take on any man in this room—especially after I show you some tricks I learned in the marines."

Any man except Tony Griffin, Delia added silently. She had a hunch not too many people ever got the best of him. That was probably one reason he'd been so acrimonious about the assault that had injured him. He had finally accepted some of the blame, but not at first.

"Now, suppose a guy comes at you with a knife in the middle of a crowd...." Tony began, using a volunteer from the class to demonstrate. "You would never want to draw your gun—it's much too dangerous for innocent bystanders. That's why you have to learn to block the attack using only your brains and your brawn." Instructing his volunteer to feign a knife attack, Tony demonstrated several techniques for blocking blows and disarming the suspect.

Following his instructions, Sylvia blocked Delia's repeated attempts to "stab" her. When they reversed roles, Delia tried to do the same, but for every defense, Sylvia had a countermove.

"I'd be dead three times over," Delia groused.

"Relax, it's just the first day," Sylvia said on a laugh. "Look. When I do this, you do this. See?" She showed Delia how to sidestep the blow and use leverage to throw her attacker off balance.

She tried the technique several times. When it finally worked, she clapped her hands in triumph.

"See, you'll catch on. Now, let's go back to that basic blocking move Sergeant Griffin showed us."

Tony walked among the recruits as they practiced, correcting one man's stance, another's arm position. But his attention was never far from Delia. Damn, he'd almost succeeded in wiping her seductive memory from his mind, but seeing her again brought it all crashing back—the silky texture of her burnished-bronze hair, her willing response to his touch, the sweet smell of her. She had that wholesome, healthy, inner sort of beauty that shined through no matter what—even when she was seething at him.

When Tab Shenniker had suggested the teaching job, Tony's first thought was that he would encounter Delia again. It occurred to him that Shenniker was thinking the same thing. The chief had made no secret of his adamant opposition to Delia's training. With Tony in place as the defense instructor, Shenniker would at least have someone keeping an eye on his precious niece.

Despite some misgivings, Tony had asked for and received the position. He was plenty qualified, with a black belt in judo and years on the street handling drunks, wigged-out junkies and just plain old ornery people. If he could handle them, surely he could handle one pint-sized female, even if there was a powerful physical attraction involved.

When his casual tour of the class led him to Delia and her partner, he couldn't make himself walk on past. Instead, he paused to watch, fascinated, as Syl-

via Mendez instructed Delia to widen her stance to give
herself more stability. She was exactly right, although
Tony suspected that no matter how Delia stood, a
strong wind could still topple her. She was so delicate.

"You have some experience in self-defense, Mendez?" he asked.

"Yes, sir. I was in the marines."

"Then you can probably show me a thing or two."

"Oh, I doubt that, sir."

Like hell. She could probably flatten him. "Keep up
the good work. Set an example for all the cream puffs
in here." He threw Delia a meaningful look before
strolling away.

Behind him he heard her mutter, "Cream puff, indeed!"

"Well, that's what you are," Sylvia added.

When Tony returned to the front of the class, he
demonstrated how to throw an assailant to the ground,
using a combination of judo and street-fighting techniques. "This is a variation of a judo throw called *tai
otoshi,*" he said as he extended one leg behind him and
neatly rolled his volunteer across it and onto a mat.
"It's effective no matter what the size of your oppo-
nent, because you're actually using his weight to do
the work for you."

When some of the recruits expressed skepticism, he
decided he would have to prove it to them. He dismissed his first volunteer, then searched the class for
another—a small one, this time. His gaze inevitably
settled on Delia. Did he dare? Even as he cautioned
himself not to play with fire, the words were out of his
mouth. "You, Pryde. Front and center."

"Me?" she squeaked. But she stood and joined him on the raised platform without too much fuss. Apparently she was learning something about obeying orders.

"After a few minutes of instruction, this rather *small* recruit will be able to throw me to the mat—without my help."

Delia looked up at Tony with those big blue eyes, reminding him of a small, defenseless mouse cornered by a cat. His heart danced around in his chest, and he conceded that this probably wasn't the best idea he'd ever had. But he was stuck with it now.

"Say I'm coming at you like I'm going to punch your lights out," he said. "Instead of stepping away to dodge the blow, duck your head and step closer. At the same time, turn away so that your shoulders are against my chest, and grab my upper arm."

Delia awkwardly followed his instructions. With her warm body pressed up against his, his brain short-circuited. *Bad idea, Griffin.* Why had he done this to himself?

"Okay, what next?" she asked.

"Uh... oh, yeah. Flex your knees and throw your right leg out and back. No, don't leave it dangling in the air. Plant your foot way back there." He grabbed her leg right above the knee and forced it into the correct position. Her skin was as smooth as he remembered, the underlying muscles firm. He allowed his hand to linger on her thigh for a heartbeat longer.

God, she felt good.

"Now what?" she asked, her impatience obvious.

"Now just lean forward and roll me over your leg."

"Like this?" She did as he directed, and he dutifully somersaulted over her leg and onto his back.

"That's it." He pushed himself off the mat and stood. At the same time he tried to shake off the lustful thoughts that threatened to embarrass him. But every time he looked at her, he felt something heavy and hot stir deep inside him.

Somehow he managed to marshal enough concentration that he could demonstrate to the class how to avoid injury when being thrown. The students practiced falling to the mat several times before Tony allowed them to attempt the simple throw.

He turned back to Delia. "Let's try it again. Faster this time. All in one fluid movement."

They went through the maneuver four more times, until she seemed fairly comfortable with it.

"Okay, now I'm going to offer a little more resistance."

The next time she attempted to throw him she didn't succeed. Though she tried mightily, as untrained as she was it was easy for Tony to keep her off balance.

"Come on, don't give up," he coached. "Get under me. Push your hips against mine. Use my resistance against me." He grabbed her around the middle with his free arm and tickled her.

"Hey, that's not fair!"

"Bad guys don't play fair. Concentrate. You can't let anything distract you. Come on, you can—ouch!" Abruptly Tony found himself flat on his back. A smattering of subdued applause rose from the class.

Tony leaned up on his elbows and cast a withering glance in Delia's direction. "Although Pryde's technique was effective, I don't recommend biting as a viable means of subduing a suspect. You might catch something."

Delia grinned down at him, obviously pleased with herself.

Tony narrowed his eyes, and in a split second her triumphant expression turned to one of surprise as he used his leg to whisk her feet out from under her. He caught her an instant before she would have hit the mat with a *wham,* then let her down gently, making sure he had her arms pinned.

"That's another lesson for you," he said to the class. "Don't ever let your guard down, even after a suspect is handcuffed. Anything can happen."

Tony had never seen blue eyes look quite so hot before. "That was a rotten trick," Delia said, softly enough that only he could hear.

"The streets are rotten, Pryde," he said as he released her. He stood and offered her a hand up. She ignored it. He shrugged and looked over the class. This time he picked the largest man in the room, a hulking wall of muscles who probably had a hundred pounds on Tony. "You, Crawford," he said, reading the name on the T-shirt. "Up here. Pryde, you can spar with Robertson."

Delia nodded and stepped down from the platform to join her new partner. Tony watched her go with mixed feelings. Had he been too tough?

Shenniker had told him in no uncertain terms not to give his niece any slack. The chief was obviously hoping she would get discouraged and quit. But that wasn't the only reason Tony was giving her a hard time. He wanted her to know up front that police training wasn't like studying for a master's degree at SMU. He wanted to be sure she understood that the next twenty-eight weeks would be the most difficult, physically and mentally, that she'd ever been through.

Tony showed the recruits one more move, a defensive technique for breaking a suspect's grip on a wrist. Then he dismissed them. As they milled toward the exits, his eyes sought out Delia. He felt compelled to talk to her, to assure her that he hadn't meant to embarrass her, if indeed he had. He also wanted to wish her good luck with her training. He could almost say the words and mean it.

There was so much unsettled between them. All he wanted was to leave the door open a crack. But Delia was engrossed in conversation with Sylvia Mendez, and she never looked up.

"Ah, hell," he muttered. Why was he even bothering? Her hostility toward him was clear enough. They might have had some good times together, if only she didn't insist on trying to become a cop. But as long as she was in training, they would butt heads at every turn.

When she quit... Now there was a thought. And she would quit, he was pretty sure. He'd seen her kind before. She had high ideals, but not enough grit to go with them. She wouldn't last. And when she dropped out, he would magnanimously resist the urge to say, "I told you so." He would simply offer his comfort, maybe help her decide what to do with her life. She would be penitent, and grateful and—

"You know her?" It was Rex Brown, the physical training instructor. "Can't blame you for staring. She's got a great tush."

"Was I staring?" Tony asked mildly, though inside he was seething at the man. How dare Rex lust after Delia? That was a privilege Tony reserved for himself.

"With your tongue hanging out."

"Yeah? Well, she's off-limits. She's Chief Shenniker's niece."

"Oh. 'Nough said." Rex didn't work under Shenniker, but few who'd been with the Dallas PD for long had failed to hear of him and his infamous temper.

Delia could feel Tony staring at her, but she pointedly ignored him as she joined Sylvia on the way to the women's locker room. She was still steaming over the way he'd deliberately picked on her.

"Hey, Sylvia, I changed my mind," she said.

"About what?"

"About you showing me some stuff. I felt like a total wimp today. I'm probably the smallest, weakest one in the whole class. I'll need to work twice as hard as anyone else to pass."

Sylvia smiled. "Now you're talking. How 'bout we set up a regular schedule—say, three times a week at the end of the day. I was thinking of doing extra workouts, anyway, to get rid of the weight I've gained since I was discharged."

Delia smiled, too, and for the first time that day she felt optimistic. Next time she sparred with Tony, she would show him a thing or two. She might be a cream puff now, but in a few weeks she intended to be one tough cookie.

Tony leaned on the half door of a closet-sized room, facing out toward the Southeast Station's front desk. Nothing was going on. Like Tony, the public service officer manning the desk drooped with sheer boredom.

Tony's teaching responsibilities at the academy unfortunately didn't occupy his entire shift, so until four o'clock he was standing in for the equipment officer who had resigned the week before.

The third-watch officers would finish with detail soon, and then the men and women would line up at Tony's door to receive their shotguns, radios and the keys to their patrol cars. Until then, there wasn't much to do except count the floor tiles—and think about Delia.

After two weeks of seeing her every day, she was never far from his thoughts. Even when she was wearing those shapeless shorts and a too-big T-shirt, he couldn't miss the lush curves of her body. He also couldn't help remembering that first encounter, and wishing it could have been more. In one night he had unexpectedly learned what sex was supposed to be. With Delia, it wasn't just a physical outlet, a mutual satisfaction. It was a crashing together of feelings and desires and sensations, something that felt like an awakening of his soul.

Tony squeezed his eyes shut and opened them again. He was going stir-crazy, that's all it was. He and Delia had shared one fantastic night. It was only natural for him to want to repeat the experience. That didn't mean he had to make more of it than it was.

"Afternoon, Tony."

Tony nodded at Chief Shenniker as the older man sauntered toward the equipment room. He dreaded what would come next—the obligatory progress report.

"So, how was she today?"

Tony didn't have to ask who Shenniker was talking about. "Determined as ever."

"She's not tired of it yet?"

"She's tired, all right," Tony said. "These first two weeks have been hard on her, no doubt about it."

"Well, are you being tough on her?"

"I'm tough on all the recruits." And that was as far as he would go. No matter how broadly Shenniker hinted, Tony wasn't going to single Delia out. Since that first day he had made it a point to spar with one or two different students during every class. Delia's turn would come up again, in the normal course of things, but he wouldn't push it.

"Is she learning anything?" That was the first time the chief had shown any concern for Delia's progress, other than whether she was close to quitting.

"She has a long way to go," Tony said. "But she's trying awfully hard."

"You don't actually think she'll complete the training, do you?"

For the first time, Tony wasn't positive Delia *would* quit. "Well, I did catch a glimpse of her in the weight room yesterday. On the bench press she pooped out after about three lifts."

Shenniker laughed humorlessly. "She never was much of an athlete. Oh, she tried. I remember when she was a freshman in high school she announced she wanted to try out for the girls' basketball team. Even if she'd been taller than five-foot-nothin', she couldn't make a basket if her life depended on it. What else do you hear?"

"Not much. But she's hardly started yet. After a few more weeks of that grueling academy schedule she won't be so gung ho."

"Hmph. You think it'll take that long?"

Tony shrugged. He felt undeniably guilty, wishing so strongly for Delia to fail. "What if she does make it through?'' he asked, voicing the fear both men harbored.

Shenniker grimaced, mirroring Tony's own thoughts. "Have you tried talking to her... man to woman? I mean, you did sleep with her."

Tony's collar felt suddenly tight. He gulped before he answered. "Begging your pardon, sir, but that's all over. She wouldn't listen to me. But maybe you should talk to her again. She has a lot of respect for you."

The older man's face hardened. "No, I'm done talking to her. The girl's head is thick as a brick, at least when it comes to this. She won't listen to me, never mind that I plucked her out of a slum when she was a child and probably saved her life. I fed and clothed her, put a roof over her head, bought her the best education that could be had—a master's degree in chemistry, you ever hear of such a ridiculous thing for a girl to have?

"Maybe I shouldn't discourage her from the police academy," Shenniker muttered to himself as he walked away. "If she quits, who knows what fool thing she'll do next. She might join the Peace Corps!"

Tony's thoughts were still on some of the strange things the Chief had just revealed—*plucked her out of a slum?* Tony knew that Delia's uncle had raised her, but he'd assumed that, whatever circumstances had led to that, she'd had money and privilege all her life. And a degree in *chemistry?*

He really didn't know her at all, but damned if he didn't want to.

Seven

Delia sat alone on a bench in the women's locker room, taking advantage of a rare few minutes of free time to go over her notes on criminal statutes. An important exam was coming up in a couple of weeks, and she was trying to get a jump on her studying.

She had learned more about Texas law in the past three months than most attorneys learned in three years of law school—or at least, it seemed that way to her. Her brain seethed with the facts she would need to know for the state exam.

She wasn't too worried about passing. As much schooling as she'd had, studying and passing tests came naturally to her. It was those other aspects of training that intimidated her.

The curriculum had gotten tougher lately. Two weeks ago, Delia and her fellow recruits had begun driving and firearms training. Because of competition for space on the driving track and at the pistol range, she sometimes had to report for class at four in the morning.

Her marksmanship was miserable—there was no other word for it. Yesterday, to simulate the exertion of a street chase, her shooting instructor had made the class sprint around the target range, then drop to the ground and do several push-ups, *then* pick up their guns and shoot at the targets. Her aim and technique had been so poor that the instructor had told her outright that she would have to show dramatic improvement if she expected to pass.

Her performance during high-speed driving drills, which involved maneuvering a fast, powerful police car through rapid turns, quick acceleration and abrupt braking, wasn't much better. She knocked over more cones than she left standing.

The running, calisthenics and defense-tactics classes continued every day without a break. Thanks to Sylvia's tutoring, Delia's fitness had markedly improved. She could run three miles without any problem and do sit-ups and push-ups by the dozen. But her hands were weak, by police standards. Even now, she absently squeezed and released a hand grip as she studied.

"Hey, girl, I thought I might find you in here."

She looked up, awarding a smile to Sylvia, who had become her personal coach, cheering section and best buddy. "I needed a few minutes alone," Delia explained.

"I know what you mean," Sylvia said as she straddled the bench opposite Delia. "That's one of the toughest things I faced in the marines. I hardly ever had time to—Pryde, what happened to your hands?"

Delia looked down at the ring of blue-and-purple marks that circled her wrists. "I did that yesterday when we were practicing handcuffing each other. It's not as bad as it looks. I bruise easily—like a peach, my uncle always said. You should see my other bruise. Remember when we were working on quick stops at the driving track and Carson threw the door open and knocked me flat on my..."

Sylvia winced. "I knew that hurt when it happened. But you didn't say a thing. You're tougher than I first gave you credit for."

Tough? Delia had thought her tailbone was broken, and she'd wanted to sit there on the pavement and cry like a baby. Only her wounded pride had prevented her from tarnishing her reputation any further.

The other women cadets straggled in to get ready for the morning run. Delia stood, stretched in a vain attempt to get rid of the stiffness in her body, then put her books away in her locker. Another day to get through—thank God it was Friday. One more session with Tony and she could coast through the rest.

Oddly, as difficult as her training was, her defense tactics classes were the worst. By now, she would have thought the effects Tony had on her, emotional and physical, would have diminished. She'd had no further close encounters with him. But if anything, her feelings had grown stronger.

Just the sight of him sent the breath whooshing out of her lungs, and she didn't have that much breath to spare, not after calisthenics.

Today was no different. After the requisite sit-ups, push-ups and squat-thrusts, Delia sat on the floor, still trying to loosen up her beleaguered muscles by lean-

ing over her outstretched legs and touching her toes.
All the while, her eyes followed Tony's progress as he
ambled toward the front of the class. He glanced her
way, held her gaze for a split second, then turned
away. An invisible fist clutched at her chest.

"You gotta bad case for that guy, don't you,"
whispered Sylvia, who was doing calf stretches close
by.

"What? Don't be ridiculous," Delia said quickly—
too quickly. "I mean, he is good-looking. You can't
blame me for staring, can you?"

"It's more than staring. You wear your heart right
on your sleeve. What was he to you?"

"I—nothing. It was *nothing.*"

"Bull."

"Please, Sylvia, I can't talk about it." Delia swal-
lowed back the tears that threatened. The situation
was worse than she thought, if she could still cry about
it after all these weeks. She and Tony had unfinished
business—that's what the problem was. They would
have to talk, clear the air, if she was ever going to put
it all behind her.

"Okay, if that's the way you feel," Sylvia said with
a sulky pout.

Delia felt wretched. After all Sylvia had done for
her, to shut her out seemed so unfair. "Look, I just
need to sort something out," Delia said.

"Sounds like maybe you need to talk to *him* instead of me."

She nodded. Yes, that was exactly it.

"Well, if you do need a sympathetic ear..." Sylvia
was obviously brimming over with curiosity.

"Your ear will be my first choice. I promise." Delia assured her.

Tony loudly cleared his throat and stared pointedly in their direction. "Pryde, Mendez, since it appears you're having trouble paying attention, why don't you both come up here and help me with today's demonstration."

The rest of the class snickered as Delia and Sylvia dutifully came forward to where Tony presided. This was the day Delia had dreaded. She'd known her number would come up again sooner or later. Tony had sparred with every recruit over the past few weeks, some of them two or three times. Today it was her turn.

"We're going to work on some two-on-one defenses," Tony said. "Slime often travels in pairs, and there may come a time when two attackers will try to get the best of you. It's trickier to neutralize two than one, but not necessarily impossible if you keep a cool head."

A cool head? How was that possible, Delia mused uncomfortably, when she could almost feel the heat rising from her skin? Standing so close, she could smell Tony's clean, manly scent, the one she remembered so well. It brought to mind the soap and shampoo she'd used in his shower, which brought to mind his slick hands working lather over her skin, steam swirling about them, wrapping them in a warm cocoon—

"Pryde! You with me?"

"Yes, sir," she answered automatically, although for a moment the fantasy had been so vivid that she'd tuned out the real world.

"You okay?" he asked under his breath.

She didn't know what to make of his concern. "I'm fine," she murmured. "What could be wrong?"

After giving Delia a long, uneasy look, he instructed her to come at him with a rubber knife while Sylvia grabbed him in a headlock.

"The hardest decision is which assailant to work on first," Tony said. "Generally, you want to neutralize the one with the best advantage—in this case, the one with the knife. Since Mendez has control of my upper body and one arm, I have to use what's left—the other arm and my feet. Okay, Pryde, come at me."

Forewarned of his strategy, Delia rushed him. He lifted his foot, aiming for her midsection. She grabbed his ankle, neatly sidestepped the blow and brought the knife to his throat.

"You're dead, Sergeant Griffin."

They held each other in an obscene parody of a lover's embrace, staring at each other as seconds ticked by. The brightness of anger she saw in his black-coffee eyes startled her, and in an involuntary reflex action she pulled back. She'd thought to impress him with her clever maneuver, and had actually expected some sort of praise. But apparently she'd committed a tactical error. She had made him look bad in front of the other recruits.

The silence in the room was so profound, all Delia could hear was the pounding of her own heart.

"You've been practicing," Tony said as he slowly released his grip on her.

"With me," Sylvia said. Although she still had a loose arm around Tony's neck, Delia had all but forgotten she was there.

"Ah, the dynamic duo," Tony said, regaining a bit of his humor. But that dangerous light still shone in his eyes. "All right, you two, let's do it again. We'll go slowly this time, so everyone can see what you did."

And so you can figure out how to defend against it,
Delia added silently. She had his number.

They went through the maneuver several times as
the rest of the cadets, in trios, imitated the demonstration. Several called out suggestions for how to
counter Delia's move. Still in slow motion, Tony tried
a few different tactics, with varying degrees of suc-
cess.

"Okay, let's try it full speed again," he said.

Delia didn't miss the unmistakable challenge in his
voice. She took a deep breath and then charged, ready
for anything—except what he did, which was to make
his body go completely limp. As he dropped toward
the floor, Delia narrowly missed stabbing Sylvia, her
own partner in crime, with the rubber knife. Then she
found herself flying and twisting through the air,
landing with a bang on the mat. Her head snapped
back, and for a few moments she saw a laser show ac-
companied by bells.

"Pryde? Hey, Pryde? You okay?"

No, she was not okay. He'd knocked all the breath
right out of her. On top of that, she'd landed on her
sore tailbone. If she'd been able to talk, she would
have told him what she thought of his caveman tactics.

"Say something. Are you hurt?"

As she gasped in a couple of breaths, her blurred
vision slowly focused on Tony's face, inches from her
own. The light of anger was gone, replaced by a worried frown and blatant remorse. It was the remorse
that saved his hide. He was kneeling over her in a very
vulnerable position. If he'd shown even a hint of triumph, she would have raised her knee and . . .

"Pryde, I know what you're thinking," Sylvia said. "Don't do it or they'll kick you right out of the academy."

Delia glanced over at Sylvia, who had read her mind so accurately. She could have almost laughed at the look of grim warning on Sylvia's face. But the laughter didn't come. Instead, tears filled her eyes.

"Delia, honey, you *are* hurt," Tony said in an agonized voice, using her given name for the first time since he'd become her instructor. "Where? Your head? Your back? Do you need a doctor?"

It was her bottom that hurt, although she wasn't going to admit that. Anyway, she didn't think anything was broken. She struggled to sit up, fighting for every breath. Tony's concern had won him a few points, but she was still mad. The degree of force he'd used on her was in no way appropriate for a sparring situation, particularly when he was a black belt and she was nothing.

"Don't...you...*dare*...call me...honey," she managed as she pushed his hand off her shoulder.

Tony scooted a few inches away from Delia, treating her with the caution he might show a spitting, growling cat. Her venom shouldn't surprise him, he thought. She had every right to be furious.

"Why don't you sit out the next few minutes," he suggested in his most conciliatory voice.

"I'll do that." She wobbled to her feet, then walked away with careful, mincing steps.

Tony turned to Sylvia. "Keep an eye on her, huh?"

Sylvia nodded. She didn't show her feelings the way Delia did, but Tony knew he hadn't earned any brownie points with her this day.

"So, I guess I need a new victim—er, I mean, volunteer," he said to the class. No one laughed. No one volunteered, either. Apparently Delia's fellow recruits felt just as protective toward her as he did. As he *usually* did, he corrected himself.

He found it nearly impossible to concentrate during the remainder of the class. Guilt gnawed at his insides, and every time he glanced over to where Delia sat on the floor against the wall, observing, the guilt grew until it felt like a dragon in his belly.

He wanted to apologize. He really, *really* hadn't meant to hurt her. But his pride had taken a beating when the two women had outmaneuvered him. He'd been so intent on not letting Delia get the best of him again that he'd put a little too much energy into his efforts.

For all Delia's increasing skills, she was still small. How could he have forgotten that, slamming her into the mat as if she were a sack of cement?

He dismissed the class five minutes early. Delia tried to make her escape, blending in with the others as they headed for the water fountain. Like a sheepdog, Tony cut her out of the pack, standing directly in her path.

"Yes?" Her crystalline blue eyes flickered with suppressed hostility.

"We need to talk."

She crossed her arms and shuffled from one foot to the other. "Go ahead."

"In private."

She glanced at her watch. "I don't have much time. I have to be—"

"You have a few extra minutes, because I just gave them to you. Please, Delia."

She nodded, grudgingly, it seemed, though she didn't object when he took her elbow and guided her to a quiet corner of the gym.

"Are you feeling all right?" he began.

"Fine." Her arms were still folded tightly, her head down.

"You're not dizzy or anything? That was a pretty hard knock you took on the head."

"You don't have to tell me. No, I'm not dizzy."

"You do know it was an accident, don't you?"

She didn't answer; she merely surveyed him skeptically.

"For cryin' out loud, Delia. I would never hurt you on purpose. I got carried away, that's all. My pride got in the way of my common sense, and I'm sorry."

That woke her up. "*Your* pride? Listen, I'm the one out there busting my buns day in and day out, trying to prove I'm tough enough to make the cut, trying to shake that stupid nickname you gave me—thank you very much—and you're worried about your pride?"

"What nickname?"

She looked down at the toes of her tennis shoes. "Cream Puff. A lot of people heard what you said to Sylvia that first day, and I've been stuck with it ever since."

Tony frowned. This conversation wasn't turning out the way he'd planned. "Then I'm sorry for that, too."

"Are you? I'm not so sure."

The fact that she questioned his integrity, his very character, hurt more than he would have thought possible. "Why don't you believe me?"

"Because I think you'd like nothing better than to make me quit. I think you're in cahoots with my uncle. You're making my training as hellish as possible, and you'd do worse if you thought you could get away with it. Call me paranoid, but I suspect some of the other instructors are in on it, too. They single me out for an awful lot of abuse."

At first he didn't know how to react to her accusation. He wanted to deny it. But she was partially right. He did want her to quit. And he was "in cahoots" with her uncle, discussing her with him almost every day. He couldn't speak for the other instructors, but if any of them knew of Chief Shenniker's fervent wish that his niece take up another career, Tony wouldn't be surprised if, consciously or unconsciously, they were making things harder than necessary on Delia.

"There is some truth to what you're saying," he admitted after a long pause.

She blinked in surprise. "You're not even going to deny it?"

"Not all of it, although when I threw you to the mat today, it had nothing to do with trying to make you quit. I wasn't even thinking about that. I promise, all I wanted was to reclaim my manly dignity."

He sensed her uncertainty and pressed his advantage. "Look, neither of us has time to go into it right now. You have to shower and get to class, and I have to get back to the station. Do you think we could get together this evening?" He hadn't meant to issue the invitation. His original plan was simply to get her to accept his apology. But now he found he had so much he wanted to say to her, so much he wanted to *hear* from her, he couldn't possibly do it in five minutes.

But she shook her head. "I... I don't think so. There's the state exam coming up—"

"I'll let you soak in my hot tub," he cajoled. "You might feel okay now, but tomorrow you're going to feel like you've been run over by a truck. A good, hot soak will help."

She was wavering. He could see it in her face, in her eyes, which weren't quite as crystal hard as they had been.

"I'll throw in a steak dinner."

"No, really, Tony, I don't think it's a good idea. Isn't there some rule about recruits socializing with staff?"

"This isn't socializing, it's . . . whirlpool therapy. Anyway, I'm not on staff. I'm just a substitute, and my stint here will be over shortly. . . ."

She was shaking her head. All the rationalization in the world wasn't going to convince her.

He sighed. "All right. But if you change your mind, you know where I live. I'll be home tonight, grilling steaks. They'll be ready about eight."

He walked away, giving her no more opportunity to argue.

Delia knew she was sunk. She could deny it up one side and down the other, but she was going to Tony's tonight. He had extended the olive branch, after all, and he did appear truly sorry for having manhandled her. And hadn't she decided earlier that they needed to talk, to clear the air?

"Sure, Dee," she said aloud, peering at herself in her bathroom mirror with a critical eye. If she actually believed all they would do is talk, why was she applying makeup with such exacting care? Why did she have hot rollers in her hair? Why had she tried on every outfit in her closet before deciding on one?

She could tell herself over and over that the lure of a steak dinner and a dip in the hot tub was just too hard to turn down. But it was Tony's company that she looked forward to, despite the antagonism she'd shown him this morning. After all, would the steak care what she looked like?

The fact of the matter was, she suspected—no, she *knew*—that if she went to Tony's tonight, they would end up in bed. For weeks, the sexual attraction between them had been drawing ever tighter, until now it felt like a violin string stretched to the breaking point. No matter what they were doing—sparring, arguing or ignoring each other—the awareness was there like a physical presence. All it would take was a little privacy and a little time, and the passion would explode.

Under such circumstances, it was foolish for her to accept his invitation. Making love with him again was sure to confuse her further and fill her head and her heart with problems she didn't need. Yet she would go. She couldn't stop herself.

When she stepped out of her car in front of his house at a quarter to eight that evening, she could smell the charcoal smoke. Her mouth should have watered at the thought of a sizzling steak. Lately she hadn't had time for more than sandwiches and frozen dinners. Instead, her stomach rolled.

She'd thought herself recovered from this afternoon's embarrassing incident, but apparently not. Damn, she didn't want to deal with nausea right now.

Tony's front door opened before she even reached the porch. Had he been watching for her? The thought warmed her, as did his welcoming smile, and she felt somewhat better about her decision to come. The man really did care something for her, even if he was trying to sabotage her new career.

"You're here," he greeted her, sounding amazed.

"You don't honestly think I could turn down a hot tub in my condition, do you?" she quipped as she entered his house. No sense in letting him get too confident of his irresistible appeal.

Tony watched her appreciatively as she strolled past him into the foyer leaving behind a faintly feminine, very alluring scent. He was pleased she had decided to come, although not as surprised as he would have her believe. Masculine intuition, maybe. She was an intelligent woman—most of the time—and she knew as well as he did that they could solve nothing between them without some honest communication.

Honest communication—jeez, listen to him! He sounded like a self-help book. That's what Delia was doing to him.

After she had accused him of lacking sensitivity in his police work, he had begun to review his past, scrutinize some of his decisions. He didn't necessarily believe she was right. He was still convinced that a cool head served a cop better than a soft heart any day. But the very act of self-examination was a departure for him, a clear indication that one night with Delia had done something to him.

In weak, whimsical moments, he imagined that Delia had opened the Pandora's box of his soul. Scary stuff. Scary, but maybe it was ultimately beneficial.

"You've changed something," Delia said with a puzzled frown, looking around. She distractedly set down the large leather purse she carried and took off her denim jacket.

"Mmm-hmm." As she surveyed his living room, he surveyed her, and found nothing lacking. Her black stirrup pants enhanced the slimness of her legs, and

the fall colors of her nubby, oversize sweater comple-
mented her vivid coloring. She wore her hair loose so
that it spilled over her shoulders like molten bronze.
He wanted to touch it, to allow the scent he knew it
held to fill his lungs.

"Ah, I know," she said triumphantly. "You bought
pillows for the couch." She walked to the sofa with
careful steps, her sore muscles evident, and picked up
a small yellow throw pillow to examine. "Right?"

"Mmm-hmm," he said again without elaborating.
The truth was he'd seen the pillows while strolling
through Sears on his way to the hardware department. For some unknown reason they had appealed to
him, so strongly that he'd bought four of the damn
things before he knew what hit him. It was only later,
after he got them home, that he realized the color of
the pillows exactly matched the buttery yellow of the
warm-up suit Delia had worn the night they made
love.

"Well, it's a start," she said.

He wondered just exactly what she meant by that,
but he didn't question her further. There were other,
more important things to discuss than his interior
decorating.

"So, are you hungry?" he asked. "I was just about
to put the steaks on."

"Umm, actually I'm not. But you go ahead."

"You're not?" His heart sank. He wanted to cook
for her. "Did you already have dinner?"

"No. But my stomach is a little upset. Nerves, I
guess."

"What do you have to be nervous about?" Dumb
question. She was alone with a man who lusted after

her, one who intended to have her if at all possible. She had every right to be nervous.

"The state exam's coming up," she said with a shrug.

He didn't buy her explanation. No one who willingly endured a master's degree program—in *chemistry,* no less—was bothered by a written test. But neither did he feel like badgering her for the truth. Tonight he would show her that he knew how to be a nice person, a caring person. "I'm sorry you don't feel well. There's some pink stuff in the bathroom upstairs, if you think that would help."

"Actually, a cold drink might help, like ginger ale or club soda."

"Club soda, coming right up." He tried to sound cheerful, but he couldn't help but cast a worried glance in her direction. She wasn't making this up—she did look a bit green around the gills. How was he supposed to get her to relax and talk with him if she was sick? And why was it that no encounter with her ever went the way he planned?

He poured the carbonated water over ice in a tall glass and handed the drink to Delia, who flashed him a tentative smile. "I'm okay, really," she said. "Put the steaks on. I might change my mind."

He hoped she would. He wanted to see her relaxed and smiling, so much so that he dreaded bringing up any topic of conversation that might cause tension. But he had to. That was why he'd invited her here. One of the reasons, anyway.

The coals were hot and the steaks, a couple of fat fillets, grilled quickly. Tony flipped them, then returned inside to put the rest of the dinner on the ta-

ble—two chilled salads, two baked potatoes, a loaf of
French bread and a bottle of red wine. Delia watched
with raised eyebrows as he moved from refrigerator to
oven to dining room table.

"You knew I'd come," she said.

"I hoped."

"I'm flattered. You obviously went to a lot of trouble."

He shrugged. "I bribed you to get you here. Now
I'm simply delivering." But he hadn't promised can-
dlelight. He lit the tapers in a modern, free-form can-
delabra, set it in the middle of his black glass dining
room table, then went back outside to retrieve the
steaks, wondering just what the hell had got into him.
Delia damn well ought to be flattered. He'd never
worried so much over dinner preparations.

Delia allowed Tony to serve her a steak and a potato, but she hardly ate anything. Oh, she made a big
show of pushing the food around her plate. The only
thing she really consumed, however, was bread, without butter, and a little of her potato.

"I'm sorry," she said, putting down her fork. "It's
a lovely dinner, really, and I'm not doing it justice."

"Don't worry about it. I'll wrap it up and maybe
you'll want it to—later." Damn, he'd almost said tomorrow. Okay, so he was hoping she would spend the
night. Was that so awful?

He didn't plan to put any pressure on her. First
things first—they would talk.

The meal was over. He stood and began clearing the
dishes, pinning her to her chair with a warning look
when she started to rise as if to help. "This will only
take a minute," he said. "Certainly you did enough

cooking and cleaning the last time you were here to exempt you for a while.'' With that sentence, he had subtly reminded her of their previous time together. He wasn't sure if that was very clever of him, or very stupid. Her last visit hadn't been ideal, despite the incredible lovemaking.

He risked a sideways glance at her. She didn't appear moved one way or another by what he'd said. In fact, she seemed to be caught in her own thoughts.

True to his word, the leftovers were put away and the dishwasher loaded in record time. He wiped his hands on the dish towel, which he tossed through the doorway into the laundry room. Then he turned back to Delia, who waited calmly for him in the dining room. For once she had done as he'd asked.

He blew out the candles. ''Did you bring your swimsuit?''

She nodded, her expression still solemn.

Visualizing her in a bikini, he couldn't help the smile of anticipation that spread across his face. ''Good. You can change in the bathroom under the stairs. You'll find towels in there, too. Just come out to the patio when you're done, and I'll have everything ready.''

Again she offered him that shy, tentative smile before slipping away to change. It occurred to Tony then that something was wrong—something other than an upset stomach. This was not the friendly, bubbly Delia he'd first met that cool November night. Back then, her easy smiles and overflowing curiosity had irritated him. Now he found himself searching the soulful eyes for some sign of the optimistic young woman she'd been, so brash and full of herself.

Was police training so hard on her that it had changed her forever? He hoped not. Regardless of whether she graduated, he didn't want to see her spirit crushed. *That* would be a crime.

Eight

By the time Delia reappeared, Tony was already waiting for her in the redwood hot tub. He watched appreciatively as she came through the sliding glass door toward him, although the towel draped over her arm obscured his view of her body.

"Brrr, it's freezing out here," she said as she skittered across the cold quarry-tile floor in bare feet. She quickly climbed the two steps leading up to the hot tub, sat down on the edge and swung her legs around, plunging them into the steaming water. "Ouch, that's hot."

"Are you going to complain all night about the amenities or get in the water?" he teased. He sat opposite her, submerged almost to his shoulders, his arms stretched out to either side and resting on the hot tub's edge.

"Don't rush me."

"You can't take that towel in the water with you, you know."

She clutched the towel even more tightly against her body. "All right, but you have to promise not to laugh at this swimsuit."

"I won't." No matter what the suit looked like, wrapped around Delia's body it wouldn't be funny.

Resolutely she thrust the beach towel aside. Tony got a swift impression of ruffles, hot pink polka dots and lots of smooth skin showing between top and bottom before she glided into the swirling water, obscuring herself behind a privacy screen of bubbles. Submerged to the neck, she leaned her head back and closed her eyes.

"Ohh, yes," she said, followed by a sigh of supreme satisfaction. Then she went silent.

While her guard was down, Tony made a leisurely study of her, or what he could see of her. She had pulled her hair back in a loose braid, the tail of which dangled over her shoulder and into the water. Several tendrils had escaped her hasty efforts, curling mischievously about her heart-shaped face. He noticed again the dusting of freckles across the bridge of her nose, the sweep of dark eyelashes casting shadows on her cheeks.

The expression on her face was what he paid the most attention to, however. Tense at first, the tiny muscles around her mouth and eyes began to loosen, until she looked as relaxed as she had when he'd watched her sleep in his bed.

More than anything he wanted to pull her to him and kiss those temptingly full lips, to gently massage away her aches and pains and then make love to her until she forgot whatever it was that troubled her. But first things first.

"Delia?"

"Mmm?"

"About this morning—"

"You don't have to apologize again." She opened her eyes and looked at him, forthright and frank. "I was angry and frustrated and *hurting* after it happened, but I've mellowed since then. Accidents are bound to happen during the kind of intense sparring we do."

At least she understood that it *was* an accident. "I was still wrong to take advantage of your inexperience."

"Yes, you were wrong. But you've admitted it and you apologized. I accept your apology. Now let's forget about it." She offered him a quick, forgiving smile before closing her eyes again.

He should have been satisfied by her response, but he wasn't. If she had forgiven him, shouldn't he feel as if they'd reached some sort of new understanding? He didn't. She was as distant as ever, despite the intimacy of sharing a hot tub.

"How's your stomach?" he asked, for lack of courage to make a more personal query.

"Better. Eating helped, I think."

"Delia."

"Hmm?"

"Maybe it's none of my business, but what's wrong?"

She opened one cautious eye. "What do you mean?"

"You seem unusually...quiet. Of course you're tired and your muscles ache, but if I know you at all, it takes more than that to keep you down."

She curled her legs up and wrapped her arms around them, then rested her chin on her bent knees, surveying him thoughtfully, giving him her full attention. "Do you know me?" she asked, a clear challenge.

"Not as well as I'd like to," he admitted. "But I have learned some things about you. You're basically cheerful and optimistic, curious, open with your feelings. You have a lot of energy, you work hard for what you want...and you're tougher than people give you credit for. How am I doing so far?"

"Do you really think I'm tough?" she asked, latching on to his last observation.

"In a lot of ways, yeah."

She smiled, and Tony's heart lit up in response. But the flash of her former self was all too brief. A worried frown quickly overtook her face. "Not too many people would agree with you. Tony, if I tell you something, do you promise not to repeat it?"

"Yes, of course." He was surprised and pleased all out of proportion that she would trust him with a secret, any secret.

"Especially not to my uncle."

"I promise." He moved closer to her, as if she might whisper the secret to him. In a gesture that seemed as natural as breathing, he took her hand in his, noting the ring of bruises around her wrist. Damn handcuffs. Even thirteen years after the fact he could still remember how punishing the stainless-steel Smith & Wesson cuffs felt when someone slapped them on you twenty times in a row.

She took a deep breath. "I'm thinking of quitting."

It took him several long moments to comprehend what she'd said, and then he was astounded by the effect her words had on him. He should have felt intense relief. Finally, after all these weeks, she was showing some sense. But relief was far removed from this surprising anxiety.

"Why?" he asked, genuinely bewildered. He hadn't expected this, not after she'd come this far.

"Because I'm too soft, too slow, too weak. That's all I hear from the instructors, and even some of the other recruits. 'Straighten up, Pryde.' 'Toughen up.' 'You're too soft.' 'You'll never make it.' My driving stinks. As far as shooting goes, I can't seem to hit the side of a barn. And today...well, today really iced the cake."

"You mean because I threw you?"

"No, not that. I mean later. The medical examiner came out to the academy for a lecture on how evidence is obtained from postmortems. He had these lovely, Technicolor slides and I sort of... threw up."

Tony grimaced. He could just imagine those slides.

"Actually it was fascinating—I mean, the part before I got sick," she said. "The m.e. was explaining how they could determine the exact position of a gun when it was fired by measuring the bullet's trajectory through the body, and how they can figure out from tissue samples how much of a certain drug was ingested and when. It's so exact. Since my educational background is in science I was especially interested, and then . . . I don't know what happened. Next thing I remember I was bolting out the door. I barely made it to the ladies' room."

Poor Delia. Tony's heart went out to her. She'd really had a rough day. "Did you try using my little trick?" he asked. "Did you remind yourself that the slides would look exactly the same, whether you're there to see them or not?"

"I didn't have time to use it. I wasn't even bothered at first, and then, *wham!* It was mortifying."

"You shouldn't be embarrassed," Tony said. "It's not an uncommon reaction. Back when I was in training, classes would actually tour the m.e.'s office to view an autopsy. The biggest, burliest recruit in my class passed out. It's nothing new."

"Oh, yeah? By the way everyone made fun of me, you'd think I was the first and only person to be bothered by those scenes."

"Well, you aren't. Not by a long shot."

She paused, again studying him. "Tony, why aren't you saying 'I told you so'?"

Why, indeed. After all this time, here was the perfect opportunity to convince Delia that police work wasn't up her alley. She was showing doubt, revealing her vulnerabilities. He should strike now, multiply her doubts, bring up every conceivable reason for her staying off the force. He should use any means of persuasion at his disposal to convince her to drop out of the academy.

But he couldn't quite bring himself to do it.

"I'd be lying if I said I didn't want you to quit," he said. "I'm still not sure you can cut it. But . . ."

"But? There's a 'but'?"

"I didn't think you'd make it through that first day. You proved me wrong. Then I thought it might take as much as a week to convince you to give up. You proved me wrong again. You work as hard as any re-

cruit I've ever seen. I'm beginning to think you have
the grit to make it.''

"Well, thank you," she said, looking decidedly
pleased. "From you, that means a lot. But even if I
have the grit, I don't have the skills," she added
gloomily.

"Skills are learnable. When you first started, you
couldn't spar your way out of a paper bag. Three
months later you're one of the best in the class.''

"You don't have to say that just to cheer me up."

"No, I mean it. A lot of the guys have a size advantage over you, but you're quick and smart and you
know the moves. You proved that to me today.''

"Well, I guess I am doing better in that area," she
conceded. "As hard as Sylvia's worked to whip me
into shape, I had to show some improvement. But
what about my other skills?''

"You have four months of training left. That's
plenty of time. A few extra hours of practice every
week . . .''

Of all the people Delia would have expected to en-
courage her, even grudgingly, Tony was second to
last—in front of only her uncle. She was downright
stunned.

"I appreciate your advice," she said carefully. "But
I don't quite understand why you're offering it. You
really don't want me to become a police officer. You
said that, didn't you?''

"I said that.''

"Why?''

"Because . . . hell, I don't know. I have a hard time
seeing you as a cop. No matter how you improve, I
just can't see you on the streets.''

"But why not? Of course it's not pleasant to think about the danger involved, but if I'm well trained, well prepared, what's the big deal? They won't give me a badge unless I know what I'm doing, right?"

"I sincerely hope not."

"I want to do this, Tony. I want to help people."

"There are other ways to help people," he pointed out.

"I know that. For a long time I wanted to work in the field of medicine—that's why I studied chemistry. But the laboratory seemed too far removed from real life. Finally I realized that helping fight crime is what I need to feel useful, like I'm making a difference. I've always admired Uncle Tab's work, and now I want to do it myself. You can understand that, can't you?"

He sighed. "I understand that just talking about it puts the fire back in you."

In the silence that followed he continued to simply hold her hand under the water and rub his thumb over her knuckles. The caress, as simple as it was, relaxed her until thoughts of her ambitions, her rigorous training and her uncle's disapproval migrated to the back of her mind. Slowly every nerve ending in her body awakened. She became more aware of her surroundings—the gentle rumble of the swirling bubbles, the clean smell of pool chemicals mixed with the subtle, masculine scent she'd come to identify with Tony, the steam bathing her face and forming droplets in her hair.

Tony squeezed her hand more tightly, a preface to his next words. "As much as it pains me to say this...don't quit, Delia. At least, don't quit because you're discouraged. If it's something you want this badly, go for it. You may not graduate—I'm certainly not ruling that out—but at least you'll have the satisfaction of knowing you tried your hardest."

"Oh, Tony. I don't know whether to kiss you or slug you. First you cheer me on, and in the next breath you say I'll probably flunk out!"

"Kiss me or slug me, huh?" His voice was soft and deep, brushing against her like velvet as surely as his thumb now brushed the underside of her wrist. Her pulse leapt in response. "Could I maybe sway you in one direction or the other?"

Suddenly she wanted him so badly, her whole body vibrated with the need, and she couldn't think of a single reason not to give in.

Maybe they weren't quite on the same wavelength, but this was as close to harmonious as they'd ever been. Even if he didn't completely understand her, at least he was trying.

He was opening up to her, too, in a way that would have been impossible several weeks ago when she couldn't get past his tough-guy shell. It was almost like seeing the rays of sunshine dancing behind a gray cloud . . . or like lemon-yellow pillows, lighting up his monochrome living room. It made her want to sing. Or make love. Or both.

"So, is it a kiss or a sock in the jaw?" His voice was almost a whisper now, his mouth close to her ear. His warm breath tickled her hair, making her shiver despite the steamy hot tub. She had only to turn her head. . . .

With a gentle but insistent hand to her jaw, he angled her face toward him, taking the decision away from her. Immediately his warm mouth fit over hers. He wrapped his other arm securely around her shoulders so that she couldn't escape—not that she wanted to—and proceeded to slowly explore every facet of a very erotic kiss. She opened to him, matching his excitement with her own fervor, his intensity with the white-hot fire that raced through her veins right along with her blood.

Tony's kiss eventually slowed to a series of teasing nips to her lower lip. Delia caught her breath and wondered dazedly what came next.

"I have one more point to make," he said, pausing to tickle her ear with the tip of his tongue. "Then I'll leave you alone to make your own decisions."

Decisions about what? Delia wondered. What *had* they been talking about? "Okay, make your point," she said lazily. *But hurry up,* she wanted to add. *Then kiss me some more.*

"Cops are lousy at relationships. The hours, the stress, the danger, the preoccupation with work—it's hell. I'm a cop. That's one strike against us. If you become one, too . . ."

Relationship? That brought her lurching back to alertness. "But, Tony, we don't have a relationship," she argued even as her heartbeat raced again. She was sure he could feel it, where his fingertips rested lightly on her neck against the pulse point.

"You think not?" The words were a tease, deliberately seductive.

She found it hard to think. "We . . . we spent one night together. That doesn't make a relationship."

"What if we spent more than one night together?" He trailed one wet finger up her arm, pausing to thoroughly caress the inside of her elbow. "How many would it take?"

Delia's mind teemed with possibilities even as he launched a new, more sensuous assault of kisses on her neck, just below her ear. Her muscles, already loose from sitting in the warm water, turned liquid. If Tony's arm hadn't been around her shoulders, her boneless body would have slipped to the bottom of the tub.

She made a supreme effort to overcome her delicious lethargy and collect her thoughts. "I don't have a lot of leisure time just now, you know."

"I know," he murmured. "Believe me, I know. I'll take what I can get. I won't ask for more than you can give."

"Then you really want to try?"

He stopped kissing her and looked at her, his dark brown eyes appearing almost black. "For months I haven't been able to get you out of my head. I feel more alive when I'm with you. I couldn't let you walk out of here again without trying *something.*"

Walk out? At this point, he would have to chase her with a broom if he wanted her to leave.

"I can't make any promises about how it'll turn out," he added.

"Neither can I." Even if she survived her training, she had her doubts that any relationship could. Still, a ridiculously optimistic hope burst into bloom somewhere near her heart. "Tony, I'm willing to try if you are."

He smiled broadly, without holding anything back—one of the few times Delia had seen him do that. He quickly took possession of her mouth once again. His exuberant kiss was one of celebration, of new beginnings, and she reveled in those feelings. She felt no hesitation now, no caution, just an overriding sense of rightness. She wrapped her arms tightly around him and returned his kiss measure for measure.

This time, when they made love, there would be no demons to chase away.

"Tell me," she said with a teasing smile, "is whirlpool therapy for sore muscles always like this?"

Reluctant to awaken Delia, Tony entertained himself the next morning by closing his eyes and breathing in the warm, drowsy scent of her. He could hardly believe she was here again, in his bed. If he had his way, she would come back, again and again. Her training would take up most of her daytime hours, he knew. But she had to sleep sometime, and she could just as easily sleep with him as alone.

She lay on her stomach with her arms wrapped around a pillow, the covers tangled around her legs. Her position gave him an uninterrupted view of the tempting curves of her back, the womanly swell of her hips and the ghastly bruise, larger than his open hand, that sprawled across her creamy flesh. When he'd noticed it last night, she'd explained that a previous fall had caused the original injury, so she was already sore when they'd started sparring. Still, whether he'd caused the bruise or not, he felt her pain almost as if it were his own.

Her hair was a mass of disorderly bronze curls, testimony to the fact that she had not slept calmly the entire night. Tony smiled, remembering her reckless abandon when they'd made love in the hot tub, then again in front of the fireplace and a third time in his bed. Afterward, their seemingly insatiable desire for each other subdued for the moment, she had proclaimed herself starving—for food—and they'd raided the refrigerator.

It had done him good to see Delia gobble down her leftover dinner and more, her appetite as well as her good spirits restored. She had then gone immediately back to bed and dropped into a dead sleep—a healing sleep, he hoped.

Tony gently removed the elastic band from her hair and finger-combed the silky disarray. She stirred, making sleepy murmurs, then rolled over, her eyes open and smiling.

"Morning already?" She glanced at the window, where bright sunlight tried to push its way through the blinds, and a small crease appeared between her eyebrows. "What time is it?"

"A little after nine."

"Oh, hell." She looked up at him apologetically. "I have to go."

"Go? Where?" His visions of a leisurely morning in bed evaporated.

"I have time reserved at a shooting range at eleven o'clock, and I need to get home, shower, change, then drive clear across town."

"Then you're going ahead with your training?" He felt an odd mixture of pain and relief.

"Yeah. I guess I'm not ready to throw in the towel yet. Things have a way of looking better in the morning—especially after a night like last night." Her naughty smile softened the shock of her imminent departure.

Tony stroked her cheek with the tip of his finger. "I was planning to pamper you this morning—give you a back rub, bring you breakfast in bed, run a warm bath for you." He traced her full lower lip. "Sure you won't stay?"

"Tony . . ."

"I know, I know, I promised not to ask for more time than you can give, and I'm already breaking that promise. All right. Will you let me toast a bagel for you?"

"Deal." She pecked him on the cheek, then jumped out of bed and scurried to the bathroom, as if to distance herself from temptation.

Tony threw on a pair of jeans and a sweatshirt and went downstairs to slice bagels. When Delia joined him a short five minutes later, she was dressed and obviously ready to leave, but she did sit down at the kitchen table to nibble at the simple breakfast he had prepared.

"So, what kind of gun will you be shooting at this place?" Tony asked as he poured two cups of hastily brewed coffee. "If you're going to practice away from the academy, you should work with the same sort of pistol."

"It's a nine millimeter, just like I use in training."

"Yeah? You're borrowing it from someone?"

"No, it's mine."

Tony did a double take. "You own a gun?"

"Uh-huh."

"Since when?"

"Since I moved out of my uncle's house and into my own apartment a few years ago. Don't look at me like that. I know how to use it. Uncle Tab taught me, although he wasn't too keen on the idea."

This was news to Tony. Shenniker had sure never mentioned it. "Last night you said you couldn't hit the side of a barn." Her instructor, Dennis Knowling, had said the same thing, though Tony wisely decided not to mention that.

"My marksmanship does leave something to be desired, especially when Sergeant Knowling breathes down my back. But I know everything there is to know about my own gun. At close range I would do just fine."

"You mean if there were an intruder in your house—something like that?"

"Exactly that," she said with a hardness in her voice Tony had never heard before. He acknowledged he had a lot to learn about Delia Pryde.

"Why did you buy a gun in the first place?" he asked.

She shrugged, obviously uncomfortable. "A holdover from childhood, I guess. In the neighborhood where I lived, a lot of people had guns. In my seven-year-old's mind, the ones with the guns held all the cards. They protected their own."

"Surely if there were a lot of guns..." He let the sentence trail off. Just how bad was this place of her childhood?

"People got killed, sometimes," she said, finishing the thought for him. "Usually it was when they were doing something they shouldn't have been doing—breaking into another man's house, making time with his woman...hurting someone. More often than not, though, if you had a gun, and people *knew* you had a gun, they didn't mess with you."

"But...you don't believe everyone ought to carry a gun, do you?" he asked, his tone just short of horrified.

She shook her head emphatically. "No, of course not. I was just explaining how I saw things when I was a kid. I don't believe *anyone* should have a gun unless they know how and when to use it. That's why I'm going to the shooting range. Besides wanting to shoot well enough to graduate from the academy, I've realized that as a responsible gun owner I need to sharpen my skills.''

Tony felt something was missing from her explanation. He looked at her quizzically, trying to think of what to ask her.

Delia knew he wasn't going to let it go. There was no reason she shouldn't tell him, other than he was bound to be shocked. He still thought of her as sheltered Delia Pryde, Chief Shenniker's pampered niece, and the hard reality of her early childhood would shatter that image. But as much as they'd shared, as much as he obviously cared about her, he deserved to know.

''Tony, I want to tell you about my mother.''

Nine

"Okay." Tony looked as if he was bracing himself for something awful.

Good, Delia thought, because it was pretty awful. "My mom was Uncle Tab's sister," she continued, "but she'd been estranged from the family, completely cut off, since she was seventeen and pregnant with me. She ran away with my father, and she never saw any of them again.

"My father left when I was five, and it was good riddance to him as far as I was concerned. Two years later Mom died. People said I was better off, that if things had gone on like they were I would have grown up just like her—poor and trashy. Maybe they were right. But I did love my mother, and she loved me in her own way. It might have turned out okay."

"How did she die, Delia?" Tony asked gently.

"A man broke into our apartment. He was looking for anything he could turn into drugs, and when he didn't find much, he killed her. I wasn't there. I was spending the night at a neighbor's house. But even back then I wished I'd been home, and I wished I'd had a gun 'cause I would have stopped that man from hurting my mother."

Tony looked as if something has just sucked all the air out of his lungs. "Whoa."

"*That's* why I feel safer with a gun," she finished quietly.

"I guess I don't blame you."

She took a few hurried sips of coffee before looking at her watch again. "I really have to go."

Tony hated to see her leave, especially on that note. What a horrible thing to happen to a child. To think that his sweet Delia had lived such a nightmare. . . .

"You don't have to look at me like I'm a stray puppy," she admonished as she stood and took her plate to the sink. "It all happened a zillion years ago. My social worker located Mom's family, and Uncle Tab took me in and gave me everything a girl could possibly want, including love and security. I didn't tell you so you'd feel sorry for me. I just thought it would help you understand a few things."

Like why she wanted to be a police officer, and why Shenniker was so protective of her.

"The night I met you, I thought you were a bored, rich little socialite looking for kicks, without a serious thought in your pretty head. I was so wrong."

"And I thought you were a stern, no-nonsense cop who was very good at his job," she said as she put the dishes in the dishwasher. "One of Dallas's finest, and one of its finest looking. I was exactly right." She wiped her hands on a towel and looked at her watch again.

Tony liked it when she flirted with him. "Hey, Delia, why don't I come with you today? I could use some shooting practice myself. I'll be going back on patrol duty pretty soon, and my right wrist is still a little sore."

She flashed him a brilliant smile. "That's a great idea. If I don't like this instructor, maybe you can give me some tips, show me what I'm doing wrong."

The warmth and enthusiasm of her response pleased him no end. He'd been worried she would resent his attempt to intrude on her day. "I'll put my socks and shoes on and be right with you."

Tony sat in Chief Shenniker's office, his hands tightly clasped to keep from fidgeting. Previously, their discussions about Delia had taken the form of casual chats. Today, less than a week after Tony and Delia had agreed to see each other, the chief had summoned Tony to his office in a way that made him feel like the school troublemaker called to the principal's office.

Shenniker sat behind his desk in silence, reading a memo, deliberately making Tony wait. No, this didn't bode well.

"I heard you were at a firing range last Saturday with my niece," Shenniker began.

The efficiency of the police grapevine never ceased to amaze Tony. Who had seen them? he wondered. Who had ratted? He doubted Delia herself would have mentioned it to her uncle, if they were even speaking to one another. "Yes, sir, I was."

"Why?" The single word was fired like a bullet.

There seemed no way out of this except to be totally honest. Chief Shenniker simply was not a man you could lie to. "There were several reasons. I needed to get in some target practice myself. I also wanted to see just how bad Delia's marksmanship really was. And I, uh . . . I wanted to spend time with her."

"Spend time? You mean the two of you are still sleeping together?"

"I wish you wouldn't put it quite like that, sir." Tony's face radiated heat like a blast furnace.

"What would *you* call it?"

"Well, in the first place, until last weekend we hadn't seen each other outside of the academy since November. It's only recently that we've agreed to . . . date." Inwardly he winced at the pale-sounding word. "I'm very fond of your niece, Chief Shenniker," he added. Another wan sentiment. "The fact that we're seeing each other—it isn't some casual fling. We've both thought about it a lot."

"Do you think she returns this, er, fondness?" Shenniker asked with a calculating gleam in his eye.

"I believe so. I hope so."

"And has it ever occurred to you that she might be, er, *dating* you so that you'll give her passing marks? And so she can benefit from your coaching?"

The idea was so distasteful, it was all Tony could do to keep from jumping out of his chair and launching a verbal assault on his superior, if not a physical one. "The idea has never crossed my mind," he said succinctly, with more control than he thought possible. "In the first place, she doesn't need that kind of help. She's doing great with her physical fitness and self-defense. She's shown more improvement than anyone else in the class. And I don't know what kind of malarkey Dennis Knowling is selling you, but she's not a bad shooter, either.

"But even if she was terrible," Tony continued relentlessly, "if you think Delia Pryde would use sex to buy herself a passing grade, you don't know her very well. She has a hell of a lot more integrity than that. She claims she got it from you."

Shenniker started to say something, stopped, then folded his hands and stared sightlessly at the forgotten reports on his desk. Finally, in an uncharacteristically quiet voice he said, "You're right, of course. I'm ashamed of myself for even suggesting such a thing. I guess I'm just grasping at straws, looking for something that'll make her... I don't know. Are you telling me she's going to make it through?"

"I'd put money on it. There's nothing you or I or anyone can do to make her quit. Given that, I say we stop trying to thwart her and channel our efforts into making sure she's the strongest, best prepared, smartest officer ever to pin on a badge."

Shenniker said nothing for a long time. He shuffled and reshuffled his papers, then straightened the things on his desk. His hand settled on a rather homely paperweight, which he picked up and gazed at thoughtfully before breaking the silence.

"Dee made this for me when she was in Girl Scouts," he said. "She couldn't have been more than nine or ten. Her school picture is inside, see?" He held it out for Tony to examine.

"Nice," Tony said of the pigtailed waif who grinned at him through the wavy plastic.

"Do you know about her past?"

"Some. She told me how her mother died."

"For two or three years after Delia came to live with me, she couldn't go to sleep until we'd gone through the house together and checked every window and door. She was frightened of so many things. Every smile I got out of her was a major triumph. Back then, I swore that I'd never let anything ugly touch her life again. You know as well as I do how ugly police work can be."

"But it's what she wants, in spite of her past," Tony argued. "No, not in spite of it, *because* of it. As simplistic as it sounds, I think she wants to put bad people in jail, bad people like the man who killed her mother. It's her choice. What we want doesn't matter."

"I wonder," Shenniker said, "if you'll feel the same way when one of those 'bad people' puts a hole in her head."

The older man's words hit Tony in the stomach like a cold steel fist. He'd often considered the possibility of Delia putting herself in dangerous situations, if and when she graduated, but he'd never thought about it in such concrete terms before.

Less than a week ago he could have talked her into quitting. Why hadn't he? Now she was back on track—more determined than ever. His support had helped give her the courage to keep fighting for what she wanted. If he withdrew that support now, he would lose Delia and gain nothing. She would find a way to get through training, with or without his help.

His best choice—his only choice—was to see to it that she learned her stuff. If she insisted on risking her life on the streets, she was damn well going to be prepared for anything.

"Can I go now, sir?" Tony asked.

Shenniker nodded absently, apparently lost in his own gloomy thoughts.

* * *

Delia hummed happily as she poured bottled pizza sauce onto a ready-made crust. It was the closest she'd come to actually cooking dinner in weeks. But tonight was special. She and Sylvia had both received the results of the state exam, and they'd both passed. To celebrate the landmark occasion she had invited Tony and Sylvia, her two cheerleaders, over for semihomemade pizza and jug wine.

Tony shared her small kitchen with her, chopping onions and bell peppers for the pizza topping. He looked really sexy tonight, Delia mused. Even the apron he wore over his khaki shorts couldn't diminish his blatant masculinity. He had such nice, strong legs. Now that warm weather had arrived, maybe she'd see more of them.

Of course, to see more of his legs she would have to see more of him, which was always a problem. Her schedule was incredibly tight. When they did manage time together, they usually spent it working on some aspect of Delia's training.

Spanish classes were her newest challenge at the academy, and Tony pushed her with all the patience of an army drill sergeant to learn her vocabulary and to conjugate verbs. Aside from making love—which they did as often as possible—they shared almost no leisure time together, so this evening was indeed a treat.

"I'm celebrating tonight, too," Tony said. "Next week I go back on patrol. No more boring desk duty."

"You expect me to celebrate that?" Delia asked dryly. "Since you insist on working deep nights, and weekends to boot, I'll never see you." She scooped up a pile of diced onion and sprinkled it on the pizza. "Plus, Sylvia and I will have to adjust to the new defense-tactics instructor."

"With you two in the class, he's the one who ought to be worried."

Worried. Although she didn't mention it, Delia realized she would have to adjust to something else—worrying about Tony. She'd been spoiled all these weeks and months, unconsciously enjoying his nice, safe teaching and desk duty. Now she would have to get used to the risks he would take, wondering every night whether he would make it home alive.

The only other time she'd felt that kind of concern about him was the night she'd spent as his Ride Along—first when she'd seen the mud on his face and thought he was bleeding, and second when he had actually been injured.

She distinctly remembered the feeling and didn't like it. But it was something she would have to get used to.

"I saw Uncle Tab this morning," Delia said.

"You're on speaking terms with him again?" Tony asked as he grated a brick of mozzarella cheese.

"Looks that way. I think he finally decided he couldn't hold out on me forever, scowling every time he saw me, grumbling at me whenever I called to see how he was doing. He actually asked me how training was going. When I told him it was going okay but that it was hard, he said, 'Hang in there, kiddo.' And you know what? I think he meant it."

"That is news," Tony said.

"He said something nice about you, too."

"Hah! I find that hard to believe."

"Well, he did. He said he was glad you're returning soon to patrol."

"Glad because we're so shorthanded. Glad because I'll be out from underfoot."

"That's not what he meant at all," Delia argued. "He was clearly implying that he considers you a good officer, a good sergeant, and he'll be grateful to have you back on the streets."

Tony rolled his eyes. "If you believe that, you really are a Pollyanna. I've been on the chief's you-know-what list ever since he found out I was helping instead of hindering you."

"Oh, that's just your imagination," Delia said with a dismissive wave of her hand. "He likes you. After all, you admitted right to his face we were, um . . ."

"Dating," Tony supplied with a grimace.

"Yeah, dating. And he didn't deck you." She paused, then returned to something Tony had said. "Is the Southeast Division really that shorthanded?"

"Always."

"Why is that?"

"Because of all the violent crime. High crime means more work, more pressure, more danger. There's a lot of frustration—crimes that can't be solved, crimes that could have been prevented, crack houses we close up one day, only to have them open up somewhere else the next, always one step ahead of us."

"But that's what it's all about. That's the challenge of being in law enforcement."

Tony slowly laid down the cheese grater as an ugly suspicion formed in his mind. "Delia, you aren't thinking of requesting duty in the Southeast Division when you graduate, are you?"

She laughed nervously. "Of course not. That would mean working with you and/or Uncle Tab, which I don't think is a good idea. That kind of pressure I can do without."

"Thank God," Tony said under his breath. He started to resume his grating when Delia's next words halted him.

"I'm thinking of the Central Division."

"The Central—are you crazy?" Tony exploded.

"Not the last time I checked. What's wrong with Central?"

"Central is just as bad as Southeast."

"So? Someone has to work those beats."

"Not you," he said emphatically. "It's no place for a..."

She laid down her wooden spoon with a clatter and put her hands on her hips. "Go on. No place for a... *what?*"

The doorbell rang, sparing Tony an answer. He wasn't sure exactly what he'd been about to say before he'd stopped himself. *No place for a little butterfly like you,* maybe, or something just as inflammatory that would have gotten him into gallons of hot water.

After everything, he still couldn't see Delia on an even par with the other recruits. Sylvia—now there was a top-notch policewoman in the making. Big, strong, able to curse like a longshoreman and get the best of a sumo wrestler. If only Delia were more like her....

Ah, but if Delia were like anyone but Delia, he wouldn't love her the way he did.

Oh, hell. He tried to suck the thought back into his subconscious, but it was too late. He loved Delia.

With that shocking realization, he took a fortifying gulp of the wine they'd opened earlier and went to the living room to greet the newcomer.

The first thing Tony noticed about Sylvia Mendez was that she looked different than she did in class.

Wearing a sleek black jumpsuit, her bold features
subtly enhanced by makeup and with her ebony hair
worn loose and curly to her shoulders, she was quite
attractive.

He must have been staring dumbly, because Delia
punched him in the ribs as Sylvia said, "Well, are you
going to stand there and gape or say hi?"

"Oh, uh, hi."

Sylvia winked at Delia. "I told you I clean up pretty
good. And get a load of this outfit. Size ten, can you
believe it? I've lost almost fifteen pounds."

"You look very nice," Tony said.

She preened a bit. "Thank you, Sergeant Griffin."

"It's Tony, please. As of yesterday I am officially no
longer your instructor, so let's ditch the formality.
What's in the bag?"

Sylvia clutched a worn shopping bag protectively.
"Some surprises, for later. Is that an open bottle of
cheap wine I see on the dining room table?"

Sylvia's brash sense of humor temporarily eased the
tension between Delia and Tony, so that they both enjoyed the evening. They polished off the pizza, the rest
of the wine and a quart of Neapolitan ice cream while
spinning tales about some of their more memorable
moments during their first fifteen weeks of training.
They laughed until their stomachs hurt.

After dinner, Sylvia revealed the contents of her
bag: fingerprinting equipment, blank arrest reports,
handcuffs and the video of the original *Police Academy*. Tony watched the movie while Delia and Sylvia
practiced arresting and booking each other. Now that
the Texas law exam was behind them, the class was
concentrating on the more practical aspects of being
a cop.

Inevitably the evening had to end. Sylvia left, promising to host another celebration at her house when they'd completed their training. Then Tony and Delia were once again alone.

Delia wordlessly began picking up the glasses in the living room. Tony helped, but he might as well have been a piece of the furniture for all the attention she paid him. The tension between them had returned in full measure, growing thicker by the minute. They were right back to where they'd been before Sylvia's arrival.

When they met face-to-face in the kitchen doorway, she tried to step around him, but he wouldn't let her. "C'mon, Delia, the silent treatment doesn't become you."

"It isn't the silent treatment," she said, not meeting his gaze. "I don't know what to say. It's true I still need a lot of improvement in some areas. But I thought I was doing better. Now, after all this time, to find out you really don't have faith in my abilities . . ."

"It's not that."

"Then what were you going to say? The Central Division is 'no place for a . . .' What? A sweet little thing like you? A *cream puff?*"

"Don't put words in my mouth. I'm not sure what I was going to say, and I stopped myself before I said it, okay? I was merely trying to make a point. It would be easier on you if you got your feet wet in, say, the North Central Division."

"I'd be bored. You yourself said you couldn't stand patrolling some ritzy neighborhood up north where nothing ever happens."

"If you're bored you can request a transfer."

"After two years! I don't want to wait. If I gradu-ate—*when* I graduate, I want to jump in with both feet, right where I'm needed the most."

"Have you told your uncle about your plans?" Tony asked, deliberately playing hardball. He knew even better than Delia what Shenniker's reaction would be.

His question produced a pained expression on De-lia's face, but Tony refused to soften. The stakes were high—maybe even life or death—and he would do what it took to win this argument.

"I haven't told him because he hasn't asked," De-lia admitted. "And don't *you* tell him. He's only re-cently forgiven me for joining the police force in the first place. I'll tell him . . . when the time is right."

"When? At graduation? That'll go over real well."

"You're badgering me, Tony." Since he wouldn't let her pass, she whirled abruptly, went to the sink and ran a stream of scalding water over the dishes. The steam rising from the sink could just as easily have been coming from the temper building inside her.

Was Tony so hardheaded that he couldn't learn from his mistakes? Hadn't he figured out by now that he couldn't control her to suit his own whims?

She hadn't actually decided which division she would request. The Central was a definite possibility, however, and she'd mentioned it hoping against hope that Tony would support whatever she chose. He had bitterly disappointed her. She wondered now if he'd been going through the motions of encouragement during the past few weeks simply to keep the peace between them.

Maybe his true attitude toward her hadn't changed at all. The possibility sobered her even further.

Tony came up behind her, placing his hands on her shoulders and pressing his cheek against her hair in a gesture that surprised her with its gentleness. "Delia, it's not that I don't have faith in your abilities. By the time you graduate, you'll be better prepared for the streets than any other recruit in that class, even if I have to see to it personally. But I don't care about the other recruits the way I do for you. I worry more about you because we're involved. I don't want to ever see your picture on the wall at the training center."

She knew which wall he meant; there was a hallway at the police academy that was lined with beautifully detailed oil paintings—portraits of every Dallas police officer who had died in the line of duty.

"I'm scared of losing you," he added.

His words, like those of a frightened child, took the fight right out of Delia. She turned the water off and swiveled to face him, grasping both his hands in hers. "Nothing's going to happen to me. You know I'll be careful, if only so I can come...so I can see you again." She'd almost said *so I can come home to you.*

Her words won a grudging smile from him, although she sensed this was only a temporary triumph.

The smile faded. He kissed her fast and hard, boldly thrusting his tongue into the warmth of her mouth, all signs of gentleness gone. Clearly he was staking his claim on her.

"Leave the dishes," he said, his low growl rumbling in her ear, sending a *zing* of fire up her spine. He didn't wait for her to agree. Already his hands were tangled in her hair as his mouth blazed a hot trail down her neck.

Passion overtook them even more quickly than usual. Tony's hands were tongues of flame, searing

her, branding her soul as his with every touch until all
Delia could think of was abandoning herself to the fire
storm. Her surroundings faded into oblivion as she
gave herself up to the one man who could create such
a fierce, aching need inside her—the one man who
could fill that need.

Tenderness gave way to urgency. She was vaguely
aware of her shirt buttons coming undone. Tony's
impatient tugs caused one button to pop off, skitter-
ing across the kitchen's quarry tile floor with a series
of pings.

It didn't matter. At that moment, nothing mattered
except to feel his hands against bare skin.

Roughly he pushed the shirt off her shoulders and
down her arms to be discarded at their feet. He paid
no notice to the racy pink lace bra she wore, viewing
it only as an impediment. It, too, was carelessly discarded. Neither did he see the matching panties she'd
carefully chosen with lovemaking in mind. With one
quick whipping motion, everything else she wore was
swept down her legs and away.

There was a harder edge to Tony's ardor this night,
a desperation that was both thrilling and a little scary.
In a hazy almost-delirium, Delia was half afraid she
would be consumed by the passion, that she would
disappear in a puff of smoke.

There were few preliminaries, but few were needed.
Delia felt molten inside. Her heated core clamored for
deliverance from the almost painful desire. An emp-
tiness inside her begged to be filled.

Tony's entire body was rigid with his impatience to
possess her. Delia was never sure what happened to his
clothes. They simply dematerialized, and then he was
holding her, flesh against flesh, hard against soft. The

steely length of his arousal pressed insistently against the juncture of her thighs as he kneaded her buttocks.

From behind, he grazed the sensitized flesh between her legs. The effect was so shockingly evocative that her knees gave way. She would have fallen if he hadn't been holding her. He slid one finger into the warm depths of her femininity, perhaps to test her readiness, but there was no need for such caution.

She was more than ready. She was on the verge of weeping, begging for fulfillment.

"Take me to bed," she said in a ragged voice. "I want you. I want you to make love to me."

Apparently the bedroom was not on Tony's agenda. He pushed her up against the refrigerator. She gasped at the shock of cold metal against her shoulders and hips, but the effect was not unpleasant. It was just one more sensation feeding her overloaded psyche.

He grasped her just above the knee and urged her to lift her leg and curl it around his hips. She did, opening herself to him. She rejoiced in the pure, white-hot pleasure as he thrust inside her, filling her body, filling her soul. She clung to him, chanting his name like a prayer, fearing she would shatter with the crazy things he made her feel.

She was his, totally and completely.

Fulfillment rumbled over her like a herd of wild horses. She bucked against Tony, arching her back, heedless of the tears that rolled unchecked down her face to fall on both of them.

With one final, explosive thrust he cried out, the sound a moving mixture of agony, ecstasy and release.

It all happened so fast, Delia felt disoriented afterward, almost like an earthquake victim unable to comprehend the devastation wrought in such a few, short seconds. But this devastation was to her soul. Something had happened, something besides sex.

"Oh, my—Delia, I'm sorry," Tony said as he held her.

"Sorry for what?" she managed to choke out as she eased her leg downward until her foot touched the floor, bringing her a little closer to reality.

"I was rough. I was impatient. I hurt you." He pulled away so that he could look at her, sliding his thumb over the moisture on her cheek. A tortured look crossed his face. "I've never acted like this before. You don't deserve to be treated like this, to be ravished in the kitchen by a rutting—"

"Tony!" She placed one finger over his lips to quiet him, at the same time searching for the words that would put his mind at ease. Yes, this act of love had disturbed her in a way, but not the way he thought. "You *were* rough," she said carefully. "You were impatient, but you didn't hurt me. I loved every minute of it. It's exciting that you want me so much, you lose your mind a little."

"A lot." He wrapped his arms around her and held her close for several silent moments, then released a deep, shuddering sigh. "Thank you."

"For what?"

"For understanding."

Delia left it at that, but she didn't really understand all of it. This interlude, although breathtaking, wasn't a case of simple desire. There was something else at work.

They eventually made it to Delia's bedroom, and as they lay in bed, there were no smiles between them, no languid embraces, no drowsy words of satisfaction or affection. Tony simply continued to hold her tightly, as if he were afraid she might evaporate. Even after his muscles relaxed into sleep, his arms remained wrapped possessively around her.

Delia lay awake long afterward, returning in her mind to their argument about which division she would request, going over and over the angry words. In hindsight, Tony's reaction to her announcement seemed perfectly normal. What red-blooded man wouldn't have a panic attack when his woman told him she intended to deliberately put herself in danger?

No, it was her own behavior that bothered her. When he had expressed a lack of confidence in her abilities—and he had, no matter how he'd tried to deny it later—her temper had flared out of control. Now she realized why.

Tony had only verbalized her own doubts, doubts that seemed to be growing. Even as her expertise in police skills improved, her belief in herself waned.

She wanted to work in law enforcement so badly, and when people had tried to tell her she couldn't, she had battled that much harder to succeed. But now the defeatest voice came from inside herself, a much more dangerous, insidious foe.

She hoped this was just another phase she was going through, such as the one when she'd been so discouraged a few weeks back. But what if it wasn't . . . ?

Ten

"Are you coming with me to Granny's birthday party?" Delia asked Tony as she watched him dress in his crisp blue uniform. "You never did give me a definite answer." She sat cross-legged in the middle of his bed, naked except for the sheet scrunched up around her waist. It was close to ten o'clock on a Saturday night, an unholy time to be getting up and dressed in Delia's opinion.

Tony paused in the act of buckling on his holster. "I don't know, honey. I would feel damned awkward, knowing how your uncle feels about me."

"And I keep telling you, Uncle Tab *likes* you. He made a point of issuing the invitation to both of us. He wants you there, and Granny wants to meet you."

The birthday party, in honor of Delia's grandmother's eightieth birthday, was to be held at her uncle's home on White Rock Lake the following day.

Most of the family would be there—aunts and uncles and cousins she'd paid scant attention to since she began her police training. It would be a good opportunity to renew ties and at the same time allow her curious relatives to get a good look at Tony.

"All right, I'll go if it'll make you happy," Tony grudgingly agreed as he ran a haphazard comb through his hair, still damp from his recent shower. "How come you're not getting dressed?"

"Just lazy."

"You know you can stay here and sleep if you like."

Delia yawned and shook her head. "Nope. I'll get myself in gear in a minute."

"Take your time. I'm going down to the kitchen and get a bite to eat." He brushed his lips against her forehead and fondly caressed her cheek, then gave the rest of her a lingering, regretful glance before leaving the room.

As she pulled on cotton shorts and a green camp shirt, she wondered what was going on inside that head of his. Tony had been distancing himself from her, a little each day, ever since that crazy night they had made love in her kitchen.

First she had tried to pretend it wasn't happening. Then, when she could no longer deny it, she had pushed his disturbing behavior to the back of her mind, promising herself she would deal with it when training was over. But it was getting harder to ignore. He seldom smiled, and sometimes he stared at her with the strangest expression on his face, sort of sad and wistful.

Was he getting bored with the relationship? But Delia shook her head. He certainly wasn't bored in bed, at least. If anything, their physical bonds had grown stronger over the past months. When they made love, it was the one time Delia could forget everything and lose herself in the profound revelation of Tony's touch. He continually surprised her with his immense capacity for passion as well as tenderness. But he was obviously, deliberately holding his deeper feelings far out of her reach.

Surely if something were wrong with their relationship, if he was disenchanted, he wouldn't be able to express himself with his body so eloquently and make her feel as if she were the most important thing in the world to him.

They had never talked about the future. The word *love* had never been mentioned. But Delia was in love with Tony, and had been almost from the first. Sometimes the love was so strong, so all encompassing, that it squeezed painfully at her heart. And loving him made it that much more difficult to accept that, whatever troubled him, he couldn't trust her with it.

A battle waged inside Delia. Her instincts told her to confront him and get the problem out in the open. Her common senses urged caution. If she pushed him into admitting he didn't return her feelings, if he told her he wanted to end the relationship, she wasn't sure how she would handle it. She had a sneaking suspicion she might just fall apart, jeopardizing her chances of graduating.

Delia had little doubt that she *would* graduate. She was much more worried now about what would happen when she completed her training.

Early on she'd been determined to jump feetfirst into a high-crime sector. But the closer she got to actually working on the streets, the more her determination wavered. It wasn't the danger that scared her. It was the responsibility, the idea that human lives might depend on one split-second decision, one hair-trigger reaction.

Soon she would have to choose between the challenging, more dangerous duty of the Central Division, or the safe-but-routine North Central.

There was a third option, she reminded herself. There were numerous civilian jobs with the police department that would well suit her talents. She could become a technician with the Physical Evidence Squad, or a statistician with Crime Analysis. Either would combine her scientific education with her new-found crime-fighting knowledge, and she would still be helping to catch and convict criminals.

On the downside, if she sought that kind of job, she would have to "demote" from police officer to public service officer. She wouldn't be able to call herself a cop, and that meant compromising her goals. But neither would she be holding lives in her hands.

She would also be out of danger, which would make Tony turn cartwheels. That was why she hadn't mentioned it to him. She wouldn't get his hopes up until she came to a firm decision.

One more month. Four weeks. In four weeks her training would be over, her choices made, and she could concentrate on Tony. Surely they could hold out for that long.

"This is where I grew up," Delia said brightly as Tony pulled his car into the driveway of the huge, white-brick colonial that had once been her home. She knew her Uncle Tab's house was impressive, indicating to anyone who saw it that she had been raised not merely comfortable, but wealthy. She glanced at Tony to gauge his reaction, but his dark eyes hardly flickered.

"What a perfect afternoon!" she tried again as they got out of the car. It was one of those warm, dry June days that begged for outdoor activity. Puffy clouds inched across the crystal-blue sky like a languid herd of sheep. "I'm so glad the weather cooperated."

"Mmm-hmm," Tony agreed absently.

What did it take to move him? Delia wondered irritably. He'd been taciturn before, but today took the cake. She'd hardly gotten three words out of him since he'd picked her up fifteen minutes ago. The only indication that his brain was functioning at all was the small but noticeable jaw muscle that twitched almost constantly.

Despite his perpetual frown, she was determined to enjoy herself on this rare afternoon of leisure. So she pasted a smile on her face, took Tony's hand and led him around the side of the house and into the backyard, where Granny's party was in full swing.

Her uncle spotted them immediately and hustled himself over to greet them, offering a kiss on the cheek for Delia and a hearty handshake for Tony. Tab seemed genuinely pleased to see them—both of them. He really did like Tony, no matter what differences of opinion they'd had in the past.

The rest of the Shenniker clan converged, welcoming Tony into the fold. The next thing Delia knew, they were both seated at a picnic table with plates in front of them, overflowing with barbecued ribs, beans and potato salad. She was pleased by the unquestioning warmth of her family, but not surprised. Years ago they had accepted her just as easily.

Again she surreptitiously observed Tony, but he showed no reaction other than polite nods and an occasional, murmured "Nice to meet you" or "Thanks."

Her family would think she'd taken up with a real winner. He showed all the charm of a toadstool.

She would have liked to attribute his broodish manner to nerves. But she knew deep down that something else was bothering him. If only he would open up to her!

Rather than making any more fruitless attempts to draw Tony out, Delia focused her attention on her uncle and couldn't help smiling. The change in him during the past several weeks was nothing short of astonishing. Once he'd finally accepted the idea of Delia joining the police force, he had embraced it wholeheartedly. Now he strutted around like a peacock telling any of the thirty or so guests who would listen that his "little Dee" was going to be a cop and walk in his footsteps.

"You want another piece of that apple pie?" Delia asked Tony. Impersonal conversation was better than no conversation at all.

He surprised her with a grin, although the slight lift at the corners of his mouth appeared forced even as he rubbed the back of her hand where it rested on his forearm. "Delia, if one more person puts one more thing on my plate and I eat it, I'll explode."

"I guess that's a no." She pushed her own plate aside after having only picked at the food.

They had the table to themselves, as most of the other guests were engrossed in a highly unorthodox Nerf volleyball game. Even Delia's granny had joined in, leaning on her cane with one hand and with the other, batting ferociously at anything that came near her.

"So, what do you think of Uncle Tab's attitude adjustment?"

"I think you must have brainwashed him," Tony answered matter-of-factly. "A few weeks ago he was so glum over your chosen career that he almost burst into tears at the mention of it. Now he's bragging that the Shenniker family is going to build a police dynasty in Dallas."

Tony's rather lengthy speech was encouraging. "The change is pretty miraculous," Delia agreed. "But I didn't brainwash him. He just decided to make the best of the situation and go with the flow. He says you're the one who told him to do that."

"I seem to remember saying something like that," Tony mumbled.

A wistfulness wrapped itself around Delia's heart. "I wish you could follow your own advice," she said without thinking.

"I'm trying," he ground out. "But I can't lie to you, Delia. I'm not happy. I've never been truly happy with the path you've chosen."

"Then why—never mind," she said quickly. "I shouldn't have brought it up, not here, and certainly not now when I only have four weeks left. We'll talk when I'm done with training." Her voice held a silent plea. *Not now, Tony.*

"It may be too late then," he said grimly. "No, now that we've started, I think we ought to finish it."

Finish it? Delia thought with a rising sense of panic. *Finish what?* "Let's take a walk down by the lake," she said, amazed at how calm and sure she sounded. "I don't want to do anything to ruin Granny's party."

They slipped out the back gate and silently walked the fifty or so yards to the muddy lake shore. Delia found a perch on an old gray dock, but Tony didn't join her. Instead he paced nervously. So she watched the brightly colored Windsurfers out on the water and waited for him to begin.

"I don't suppose you've heard a news broadcast today," he said.

Delia's heart began to pound. She didn't like his opening line. "No, I haven't. Why?"

"An officer was shot last night."

The pounding grew louder, reverberated in her ears like a bass drum. "Did he die?" she asked, terrified of the answer.

"She. It was a woman. And last I heard she was still alive but in pretty bad shape."

"What . . . what happened?"

"She approached a car parked in a shopping mall lot, just to see if anyone was in it, what was going on—routine stuff. Before she even got close, a guy jumped out of the car and opened fire on her."

Delia couldn't help the shudder that passed through her. "Did you know her?" she asked in a small voice.

"No. She was a rookie. She worked in North Central."

North Central. Supposedly the safest division.

"Did they catch the guy?"

"The officer's partner shot him—but not in time."

A lead weight settled in Delia's stomach. Although she felt awful for the injured officer, her heart went out to the partner—the one who hadn't reacted quickly enough. That's what she feared for herself, even more than dying. The fear had never been more real to her than at that moment.

"Delia, do you remember the time I told you that whenever I let myself care too much it gets me in trouble?"

She looked at him questioningly, surprised that he'd abruptly turned the conversation in such a different direction. "Yes, I remember. We were talking about our philosophies toward police work."

"Yeah, well, I've found that principle applies outside of police work, too." He stopped his pacing and stared into the distance, unseeing. "I love you, Delia. And it's causing me all kinds of troubles."

Delia's first reaction was one of overwhelming joy and relief. Tony loved her! If that was true, then whatever other problems they had could be worked out. But one look at his face told her the problems were formidable.

"I've often thought about when, or if, you might say those words to me," she said carefully. "I never imagined you'd do it standing ten feet away from me and wearing that frown."

Her teasing didn't nudge him any closer. In fact, if anything, the frown deepened.

If Muhammad won't come to the mountain... Delia scrambled to her feet and went to him. She stood deliberately close so that she could see into his face. His dark eyes were thickly veiled, so that she saw only her own pain reflected back at her. She touched his sandpapery cheek with the tip of her index finger. "So why is loving me causing you such troubles?" she prompted. "Love is supposed to make you happy."

He closed his hand around hers and pulled it away from his face, as if ruling out any physical intimacy that might have softened him. "I don't know about 'happy,'" he said, "but loving you has been good for me in a way. You opened something inside me, forced me to feel things I've never felt. I see people differently now. I've found a balance in my job that I've never had before."

"That doesn't sound so bad."

"That's not the bad part. Delia, you've become the most important person in my life, more precious every day. But no one ever told me that love would come with such a high price. The more I care about you, the more I'm afraid something bad will take you away from me. When I think of you getting hurt, getting killed, it eats away at my insides until I can't stand it."

Ah, now it all came together. He was imagining that she was the injured rookie. "Tony, accidents happen. Cops get hurt—men, women, rookies, twenty-year veterans. Even in North Central. That doesn't mean *I'll* get hurt."

He said nothing.

She tried again. "I worry about you, too, you know, now that you're back on the streets. But I don't let that worry consume me. It's just something I've consigned myself to live with. I'll get used to it, and you will, too," she said, knowing it was a lame reassurance.

"No!" he said with a savagery that frightened her. "It just gets worse with time. Please understand when I say what I'm about to say, I'm not trying to be mean or overbearing or unfair. It's a matter of survival—yours and mine."

She had a sick feeling she knew what was coming. "Go ahead. Say it."

He turned away from her as he ground out his next words. "If you plan on continuing your training, if you insist on becoming a police officer, you'll have to do it without me. I couldn't take it, wondering whether you'll make it alive through another shift. Just the worrying would kill me a little each day. And if anything actually happened to you...that would finish the job."

Delia shook her head, uncomprehending. She must have misunderstood. He couldn't possibly have issued such a cruel, selfish ultimatum. "Are you saying that if I don't quit, you'll walk? You won't see me anymore?"

"That's . . . about the size of it."

"If you love me, how can you ask that of me? You know how much it means to me, how hard I've worked . . ." Again she shook her head, hurt and bewildered.

"I do love you, enough that I want to see you live to be as old as your granny."

"You really mean this, don't you." It wasn't a question.

"Yeah."

"Tony, you must know that I love you, too, and I'd do almost anything for you, but you're asking way too much."

"I know."

Delia waited, praying futilely that he would take back the demand. It was so unfair, unbefitting the noble man she thought she knew. But the silence between them grew to uncomfortable proportions.

Finally Tony asked, "Will you at least think about it? For me?"

She stiffened her spine and spoke the words she knew would drive him away forever. "Tony. I won't quit."

He issued a hopeless sigh. "I didn't think you would."

Her next words were borne of desperation, because she knew in her heart it wasn't what she wanted. "What if . . . what if I chose North Central?"

Slowly he shook his head. "That's where last night's shooting was. You just said it yourself—it can happen anywhere."

"Tony, listen to yourself. It *can* happen anywhere. I could get a nice, safe job as a librarian, and a shelf full of books could fall over on me and kill me."

He wasn't buying it. He gave her a look that tore at her soul, and then he turned away.

As she watched him walk back toward the house, it occurred to her that she held one more card in her hand. She could tell him about the possibility of a civilian job in Physical Evidence or Crime Analysis. If she chose that path, she would eliminate the personal risk that was so hard for him to accept. *And she wouldn't lose Tony*.

She took a deep breath, intending to call to him, but his name never reached her lips. No matter what she decided about her future, it had to be *her* decision. If she caved in to his emotional blackmail, it would maybe smooth things over in the short run, but over time she would resent the manipulation.

So she let him leave. She saw no other choice that would preserve the relationship and her pride, as well. And when he was out of sight, she cried.

Eleven

Graduation Day.

Tony had tried to forget it, but he might as well have circled it in red on the calendar. Today a certain autumn-haired, strong-willed woman he knew would be promoted from Recruit to Apprentice Police Officer, complete with badge and gun. She would be on the streets tomorrow, maybe even tonight.

He rifled through the huge mound of paperwork on his desk, not seeing any of it. His thoughts were with Delia Pryde. He didn't know where she'd been assigned, but he was willing to bet she had requested the Central Division, just as she'd said she would. He tried to tell himself he didn't care.

"Sergeant Griffin. I thought I'd find you here."

Startled from his grim musings, Tony looked up to see Sylvia Mendez standing nearby. He found a smile for her. "Officer Mendez, you're looking smart in your blues and your shiny new badge."

"Thank you, sir."

So, it was back to formality. He wondered if, since they knew each other outside of work, he should invite her to continue calling him Tony. Then he nixed the idea. He doubted Sylvia considered him a friend, not after what he'd done. Her loyalties would naturally lie with Delia.

"I'm glad you requested Southeast," he said, and he meant it. Sylvia would make one helluva fine officer. "You'll do well here."

"I hope so. Why are you out of uniform?"

Tony looked down at the jeans and T-shirt he wore. "Oh, this. I'm working with the Narcotics Division to catch some kids who're dealing drugs at a carwash."

"Sounds dangerous."

Tony shrugged. "They scatter anytime a cop car comes within a mile of the place, so some plain-clothes guys are going in to see if they can't do better than I've been able to do. I'm just going along for the ride, since I know the territory. The detectives'll take care of the tough stuff."

Uncomfortable talking about the tense ordeal to come, he deliberately changed the subject. "So how did your final exams go? Well enough, I guess, since you're here," he said, answering his own question. He laughed nervously.

"Delia came through her exams with flying colors," Sylvia said, a knowing look on her face.

"Excuse me?" For some reason, he suddenly felt like an idiot.

"That's really what you wanted to know, isn't it? She aced everything, even the fitness test. And she was great during the situation simulations . . . cool as ice.

She graduated eighth out of fifty, and would have done even better if her Spanish wasn't so lousy."

"Eighth?" Good Lord. Six months ago he never would have believed she could survive a week at the academy. He should have been there. Damn, he should have been there to see her get her badge. "She must be flying high."

"Well, not exactly." Sylvia looked pointedly at her watch. "I have to go. Detail starts in five minutes." She turned, but Tony stopped her before she could escape.

"Mendez. Just a minute. Where did Delia get assigned?"

"Mmm, I promised her I wouldn't tell."

"I'll bet she went to Central."

Sylvia still didn't answer, but she looked uncomfortable enough that Tony knew he'd guessed right.

"Go on," he said, motioning for her to leave. "You don't want to be late for your first detail."

When he was again alone, he allowed himself a soft curse. Why couldn't he just let Delia go? Although physically he had separated himself from her, he couldn't get her out of his head.

Or out of his heart.

She was like a fever that would come on a man at the most unexpected times, rendering him weak with desire. Sometimes he caught her scent on the hot, July breeze, heard her sweet voice in the rustle of summer-dry leaves, felt her soft, phantom touch when there was no one but him in his bed.

Breaking things off with her hadn't solved anything. He worried about her just as much now as he ever did. He was reminded of the little mind game he'd taught Delia, the one he'd used for dealing with ugly situations: *The scene would be just as grim, the blood just as red, the people just as dead, regardless of whether you're there to see it.* That's what he'd told her. Only now, the principle worked against him, disturbing rather than comforting. He found himself thinking, *Delia will still be on the streets, facing danger, regardless of whether I'm waiting around for her to come home.*

Had Delia been right? Could he learn to cope with the worrying? One way or another he would have to. He wasn't going to stop caring what happened to her, that was for sure.

With a sigh, he pushed the untouched paperwork aside and stood. Somehow, despite everything, he was glad Delia hadn't given in to his self-serving demands. He couldn't have lived with himself, knowing he had forced her to give up her dream. No matter how much he loved her and wanted her safe, he wouldn't want to spend the rest of his life with an unhappy, dissatisfied wife.

Wife? Good Lord.

Delia drove her car aimlessly through the streets of Dallas, willing her restless mind to shut down. It was after midnight. As exhausted as she was, she should have been able to drop into an immediate and deep sleep. But as she ambled down one street after another, the darkened houses slipping past her windows unseen, thoughts of the day's events ricocheted through her mind like stray bullets.

She'd done it. Not twenty minutes after the Chief of Police had handed her a certificate and shook her hand, she had gone to her basic-training sergeant and announced that she wanted to resign and seek a position as a civilian technician with PES—the Physical Evidence Squad.

Sergeant Merkel had been appalled. "Look, Pryde, lots of new officers feel shaky at first, but it passes," he had patiently explained. "You haven't even given it a chance."

"But what if I make a mistake?" she'd asked. "I'm not sure I can handle the responsibility."

Merkel had sighed elaborately. "You're human. Rest assured, you *will* make mistakes. There's no such thing as a perfect police officer. But trust me, you've got what it takes to be a damn good one. I watched you during the simulations. Your reactions were excellent, your decisions quick and sure."

"But—"

"Give it a week. One week on patrol. If you still feel the same, then you can resign. Meanwhile, I'll check over at PES to see if anything's available."

Reluctantly she had agreed to the sergeant's request. Now here she was, driving around with a nine-millimeter pistol in her purse on the seat next to her. Tomorrow at 7:00 a.m. she would report for her first patrol duty with her field training officer.

It was only for five days. She could handle that. The first week she was required only to observe. It wouldn't be any worse than when she'd ridden with Tony.

Tony. Now there was another problem. He was the real reason she couldn't sleep.

Delia could state with complete confidence that Tony had nothing to do with her decision to quit the force. The choice was entirely her own. But now that she'd made it, was there any reason not to tell him about it?

She smiled in the darkness of her car as she anticipated his reaction. He would be thrilled. Her career change would remove the obstacle that stood in the way of their happiness. They would have another chance...or would they?

They hadn't spoken in almost a month, since he'd stalked away from her granny's birthday party. Delia had to face the possibility that her decision to take on a less hazardous profession might not make any difference. There was no guarantee Tony would want to get involved with her again.

In addition, she still harbored a fair amount of resentment about the way he'd tried to manipulate her. Granted, he had seen his ultimatum as the only choice to make. A matter of survival, he had called it. He couldn't endure the prospect of losing her. He loved her that much.

But if he really loved her, wouldn't he put her happiness ahead of his? On the other hand, if she really loved him, why shouldn't she lay aside her pride, forget his transgression and tell him what he wanted to hear—that she was taking herself off the streets?

Damn, this wasn't getting her anywhere! She'd been driving around for two hours and had used up almost half a tank of gas, but the answer to this dilemma wasn't floating around in the atmosphere, waiting for her to grab it. The only way she would figure it all out was to talk to Tony. She would lay all her cards on the table, tell him exactly how she felt, and maybe, just maybe, they could salvage the exquisite love they had tasted so briefly.

The mere possibility gave her an adrenaline high.

A sudden impatience had her chomping at the bit. She wanted to confront Tony *now*. But it was one-thirty in the morning. He would be on duty, and there was no way to get in touch.... Yes there was!

Unless he was in the middle of something, at 2:00 a.m. on the dot he would be at Go-Go Grocers, buying his doughnut fix from Carmeline. Delia intended to intercept him. Of course, he wouldn't have much time to chat, but she could at least tell him of her decision to transfer to PES. That would give him something to chew on until they could talk at length—perhaps tomorrow evening.

She stopped at her apartment only long enough to freshen her makeup and run a brush through her hair. Then she was off to South Dallas. It never even occurred to her to be nervous about driving alone in that rough neighborhood. She was a cop now—at least for another week. She could take care of herself.

Tony climbed out of the back seat of the old Ford Fairlane the Narcotics guys had chosen to use for their undercover operation.

"We're goin' to the drive-thru across the street for some chicken," said the driver, a young detective by the name of Skates who looked all of eighteen. He'd been the perfect candidate to infiltrate the juvenile drug dealers. "We'll come back and get you."

"Sure," Tony replied with a shrug, although he wished they would wait the three minutes it would take for him to get his doughnuts.

Ah, hell, he couldn't blame those guys for being too antsy to wait around. After all the careful preparation, all the anticipation, they'd blown the operation within the first five minutes. Even out of uniform and in an unmarked car, Tony's face was too well-known in this neighborhood. The kids had scattered the moment their lookout had seen him slouching in the back seat.

You win some, you lose some, he thought as he swung open the glass door to Go-Go Grocers. "Evenin', Carmeline."

"Hmph," she replied. "Where's your uniform?"

"Doin' a little undercover work tonight. Didn't pan out, though. Got any fresh bearclaws?"

She rolled her eyes. "Don't I always? How many you want?"

"I think this is a three-bearclaw night. And milk. I definitely need some milk."

"You know where to find it," she said, nodding toward the refrigerated case in back of the small convenience store.

He turned. And then he saw her. Delia Pryde was standing not five feet from him, a tremulous smile on her face. He squeezed his eyes shut and opened them again. She was still there.

"Delia? What the hell are you doing here?"

The smile faded. "Nice to see you again, too," she said with a challenging lift of one eyebrow.

"Of course it's nice to see you. I've missed you." He was mortified that his voice cracked. "But *here?* This is not a safe neighborhood for a woman alone—"

"Oh, Tony, get off it! I'll visit any neighborhood I damn well please."

"Bravo," said Carmeline, who was watching the proceedings with interest.

"Why are you dressed like that?" Delia demanded, sounding every bit as intimidating as her uncle. "And where's your gun? Every on-duty officer is supposed to have—"

"I know, I know." Tony had no idea what to make of her mood. "It's a long story."

"Maybe she'd like to hear it," Carmeline suggested.

Tony turned and gave the plump, orange-haired woman an acid look, and she immediately started rearranging the potato chip bags by the counter.

"What are you doing here?" he again asked Delia in a softer tone of voice as he closed the distance between them. He felt a tremendous urge to pull her to him, but he wasn't sure how well that would be received. He couldn't resist at least touching her, however, and he ran his fingertips along the amber silk of her hair.

To his surprise, she didn't resist. Her eyes, crackling with blue fire only moments earlier, had softened to a dreamy color that made him want to melt. "I came here to tell you something... something I think you'll like. Oh, Tony, I—"

She didn't get the rest out. She was interrupted by the sound of a young man pushing noisily through the convenience store door, brandishing a gun almost bigger than he was.

"Everybody freeze! Hands in the air, now!"

Tony ducked behind a row of shelves and reached reflexively for his gun. Of course it wasn't there—he'd left it in the car rather than try to conceal it under his T-shirt and jeans.

"Get out from behind there!" the gunman ordered.

With a sick feeling in the pit of his stomach Tony slowly raised his hands. He hoped to hell there wasn't a long line at the KFC drive-thru across the street. It'd be nice if the cavalry showed up soon.

"Oh, Lordy, not again," Carmeline said with an almost bored air as she thrust her hands upward. "Cash register's open. Fill your pockets."

"I don't want your frickin' money," the man barked. His voice was muffled by the red ski mask he wore, but his eyes, clearly visible, never left Tony. "I want him."

"Me?"

"I am sick and tired of you picking on my operation. First you cruise by my territory every five minutes, scarin' away all the customers, and then you sic the narcs on me. You're cuttin' into my profits, and I'm going to put an end to it."

As all this went on, Delia watched with a cool, detached fascination. She was the only one who hadn't put her hands up, but the gunman didn't notice or care. Good. He didn't consider her a threat.

She wished like hell she had the nerve to dip inside her big leather purse and retrieve her gun. But on second thought, that wasn't the answer. Together, she and Tony should be able to disarm him without anyone getting hurt.

She studied the gunman. He was only a kid, maybe sixteen or seventeen, with a childish, lanky build and more false bravado than real courage. He didn't look comfortable with the gun. Delia guessed he was primarily a drug dealer, not a killer. Not yet, anyway. But apparently he intended to start with Tony.

"You stupid little jerk," Tony spat out. "You're not even smart enough to figure out when you've got the edge. You have a system that works and I can't beat it. God knows I've been trying for months. And now you're gonna blow it by killing me."

"How so?" the kid asked, cocking his hips belligerently.

"You kill a cop, and every uniform in the city is looking for you. And they'll find you."

Good, Tony, Delia cheered silently. He was planting doubts in the kid's mind. Now it was her turn.

She made a loud, snuffling noise. "P-please, don't hurt my b-boyfriend," she pleaded as she inched a half step closer to the gunman.

He rolled his eyes. "Shut her up, would ya?" he demanded of Tony.

"Delia..." Tony's voice was a growl of warning.

She moved closer still as tears rolled down her cheeks. "I'll do anything you want. My uncle has money, lots of money. You could take me with you, demand a ransom. He'd pay it without question—"

"Delia!" *Oh, shut up, Tony,* she wanted to scream. He was going to ruin everything. She blinked up beseechingly at the kid, whose attention was on her now. Apparently she'd piqued his interest. "Please?" she said in almost a whisper as she touched his shoulder.

Amazing. He still didn't consider her any kind of threat.

"I don't like rich girls," he said haughtily, though his eyes—all she could see of his face—perused her with interest. "But I know someone who does." As he puzzled through his options, his aim wavered.

That was all Delia needed. When she was sure the gun was pointed slightly away from Tony, she pounced, grabbing the kid's wrist with both her hands and jerking it downward and behind his back. At the same time she threw all hundred and five pounds of herself at the gangly youth. With a surprised *oof* he stumbled and fell across the checkout counter.

Carmeline hit him over the head with the rack of potato chips. Then Tony lunged forward and stripped the gun from the kid's hand, and together he and Delia dragged him to the ground.

"Handcuffs?" Delia asked. She was sitting on the youth's shoulders—almost on his head—while Tony attempted to subdue flailing arms and legs.

"I don't have any with me," Tony lamented. "Carmeline, call 911."

Just then another burst of activity claimed their attention. Two more young men entered the store, guns drawn.

For one horrible moment, Delia thought her life was over. These were the drug dealer's pals, and they were going to kill everything in sight. Pure fear drove the words from her mouth. "I love you, Tony," she said, loud enough for everyone to hear.

Tony had time for one surprised glance at her before one of the newcomers scratched his head and looked at the scene on the floor. "Griffin, just what the hell is going on here?"

"Find me some handcuffs, would you? I've got our drug dealer here."

"Drugs?" came a muffled objection from the youth on the floor. "Did I say anything about drugs?"

The Narcotics detectives took over the arrest. Delia crawled off the suspect's head, lurched to her feet and wobbled over to the bakery case. "How about a doughnut?" she asked Carmeline. "Raspberry filled."

"It's on the house." Carmeline smiled broadly as she selected the fattest doughnut in the case and slapped it into Delia's waiting hand. "Where'd a little thing like you learn them moves?"

"Police academy," Delia answered before stuffing half the gooey pastry into her mouth. If she didn't get some food into her stomach she was going to pass out.

"You mean you're a cop?" Carmeline asked incredulously.

"Looks as if," Delia said between bites.

"I'll say she is," agreed Tony, who had caught the last bit of conversation. He slid his arm around Delia's shoulders and gave her a reassuring squeeze. "That was nothing short of magnificent. Are you okay?"

She nodded, although she was shaking like she had the D.T.'s. She didn't care if she fell apart now. She'd held herself together when it counted, and that's all that mattered. "I thought you'd be mad at me."

"Mad at you? For saving my life?"

"For putting myself at risk."

He paused before answering. "I can't say I enjoyed seeing you in danger. But you handled the situation perfectly. Delia, honey, you're shivering. Let's get out of this air-conditioning for a minute."

They went outside and perched on the hood of Delia's white Miata while the Narcotics guys took statements. The clean-up didn't take long—not nearly as long as it had with that murder last November, Delia noted as she finished up her second doughnut.

"This one might make the papers," Tony said as the Ford drove away. "I can see the headline now. Green Police Academy Grad Disarms Gunman With Tears."

"Oh, please. Uncle Tab will throw a fit when he finds out."

"I thought he accepted your career."

"He does, in theory. But when it comes to the reality of me facing drug dealers and guns, he'll freak."

"I think he'll be proud. I know I am."

"You should be. You taught me those moves."

"I didn't teach you how to cry. You really had me going with that Academy Award performance."

"Mmm, yeah, whatever." Tony Griffin had taught her more about crying than he would ever know. But that was over now.

"Are you going to give me a ride to the station?" he asked as he threw a wad of paper napkins into the trash. "I want to get back into uniform."

"Since your narc pals left you stranded, I guess so." She hopped off the hood of her car and reached into her purse for her keys. Her hand brushed the cool metal of her gun, and she smiled. Earlier this evening, the thought of that lethal weapon in her purse had intimidated her. Now it felt . . . right, somehow, that she should be carrying it.

She opened the door for Tony, her smile lingering. As they left the parking lot, she honked and saw Carmeline wave in the rearview mirror.

"So, what did you come all the way to South Dallas to tell me?" Tony asked casually as they headed down Bexar Street toward the highway.

"Huh?"

"You said you wanted to tell me something before we were rudely interrupted."

"Oh, um, yeah." Delia gulped. How was she going to get out of this one?

"Well?"

"I, um, changed my mind."

"About what?"

"About what I was going to tell you."

"Oh." For several long seconds, neither of them said anything. Finally Tony said, "Maybe this is presumptuous of me, but I thought maybe you wanted to tell me . . . you love me."

Delia snorted, which didn't do much for Tony's ego. "No, that's not it. I mean, I already told you I love you. I broadcast it to the whole world. Those guys from Narcotics are probably still snickering." She gave a little chuckle herself.

Tony didn't share the humor. "Did you mean it?"

"Yeah." Through her lingering grin, her eyes filled with tears.

"Then why are you—for cryin' out loud, Delia, pull over before you have a wreck."

He was right—she couldn't see a thing through the multiplying tears. She turned into a closed gas station and cut the engine, then did her best to pull herself together. "It's just the aftereffects of the situation," she tried, but he was having none of it.

"Bull-loney."

"Okay, just remember you asked for the truth. I came here tonight to tell you I was quitting the police force to take a job as a civilian technician in PES."

Tony's eyes widened with patent shock, and several drawn-out seconds passed before he could react. "Let me get this straight. You're going to accept a demotion and a pay cut so you can deal with blood and bodies and fingerprints and junk? You *hate* that stuff."

"I don't hate it. I find it fascinating. I'm just a bit squeamish, that's all, but I'm getting over that."

"But why would you do it? Ah, hell, I know why. Because some selfish, inconsiderate bastard asked you to take yourself off the streets so *he* could sleep at night."

"No," she said with an emphatic shake of her head. "I was going to do it because I thought it was what I wanted. I had my own doubts about police work, about whether I was really suited for the job."

"Suited for the—honey, how can you even think that after what you did back there? I've never seen any cop do a cooler, more professional job than you just did."

She allowed herself a small, internal swell of pride. "You have a point. I did okay handling that kid. When I realized the danger, my instincts kicked into gear. I knew I had to do something, and what I did felt really right."

Tony leaned back against his door, folded his arms, and grinned ear to ear. "God, you're gorgeous. If I didn't have to get back to work . . ."

"Tony! That is hardly relevant to the conversation. I'm trying to tell you something."

"Delia, honey, I'm not dense. I get the picture. You thought you wanted to quit the force because you were afraid you wouldn't come through when the chips were down. Then you got a taste of real police work. You proved to yourself that you have twice the skill and ten times the courage of your average officer, and now you've changed your mind. You don't want to quit."

"I . . . Yeah."

"I'm glad."

"You are? But I thought you—"

"I'm allowed to change my mind, too, aren't I? If you had quit, maybe it would have saved me some worrying. But I could never forgive myself if I forced you into a decision that made you unhappy.

"Don't get me wrong—I'll still worry about you. It'll make me crazy sometimes, knowing you're out there on the streets. But, by God, I want my wife to be happy."

For a moment, Delia couldn't breathe. "Excuse me?"

"I want my wife to be happy. Delia Pryde, will you marry me?"

With shaking hands she restarted the engine and put the car in gear. She hadn't gone more than ten feet when she stepped on the brakes and looked at him. He was still sprawled in the passenger seat, arms folded smugly, a self-satisfied grin splitting his face.

"When did you decide all this?" she demanded. If he'd changed his mind, why had he let her anguish so long, thinking he didn't even want to see her?

The grin faded as he realized she wasn't going to jump at his proposal. "I only made up my mind today," he assured her. "If you hadn't shown up tonight, I would have called you tomorrow."

She raised one skeptical eyebrow, resisting the urge to throw herself at him and say *yes, yes, yes* to his question. First she had to make sure this wasn't just a heat-of-the-moment decision on his part. "You're the one who said cops are lousy at relationships," she reminded him.

"We are. Neither of us has done such a good job with this one so far. But we'll get better with lots of practice, don't you think?" He flashed her a glance full of pure deviltry, and she knew exactly what sort of "practice" he had in mind. But then he dropped his bad-boy grin. He leaned toward her and cupped her cheek. "Delia, I'll never love anyone like I do you. Whether life is long or short, I want to spend it with you."

Unable to find the words, she nodded.

"Is that a yes?"

"Oh, yes," she said on a whisper just before their lips touched. It was a hungry kiss, one too long denied and more precious for its brevity. For the next few hours Tony belonged to the streets of Dallas, but these stolen moments were hers, a prelude of the joyous reunion to come.

He ended the kiss with a teasing peck on her nose. "Guess that means I'm stuck with you."

"That's nothing new. You were stuck with me the first time we met, remember?" She shook her head as she recalled what a hopeless pest she'd been as a green, overeager Ride Along. "That was an incredible night."

"I think I can safely say this one beats it."

"Definitely. A night for the record books," she said as she threw her arms around him once more.

Inevitably she had to return to her own seat, fasten her seatbelt, and drive Tony back to the station. But she stole a glance at him now and then, and she saw in his eyes a new respect. The haunting, wistful expression was gone. She had finally won his faith.

She had renewed her own faith, too—faith in her abilities, and a new, stronger faith in the love she and Tony shared. There might still be problems. A two-cop marriage was bound to produce a few hurdles to cross. But given what they'd already faced and conquered, she was sure the bonds they had forged would survive anything.

Tony took her hand and squeezed it, and a warmth spread through her like honey. For the first time in a very long time, Delia felt truly safe, body and soul— in body, because she knew with certainty that no random crime would find her helpless and unaware. And in soul, because her heart, adrift for so long, had found the safe harbor of Tony's love.

* * * * *

V SILHOUETTE® *Desire®*

MYSTERY MATES!

Six sexy Bachelors explosively pair with six sultry Bachelorettes to find the Valentine's surprise of a lifetime.

Get to know the mysterious men who breeze into the lives of these unsuspecting women. Slowly uncover—as the heroines themselves must do—the missing pieces of the puzzle that add up to hot, *hot* heroes! You begin by knowing nothing about these enigmatic men, but soon you'll know *everything*....

Heat up your winter with:

Take 4 bestselling love stories FREE
Plus get a FREE surprise gift!